Dogs, boats, sea, cou... Berrisford's childhood ... featuring as backgroun... well-loved pony and an... ...her husband, she lives by the sea, on an island where the rolling hills, sheltered coves and rugged glens offer scope for happenings as enthralling as those that befell Skipper and his human friends.

SKIPPER

The Dog from the Sea

JUDITH M BERRISFORD

CAVALIER PAPERBACKS

CAVALIER PAPERBACKS

First published by Brockhampton Press Ltd 1955

© Judith M Berrisford 1955

Published by Cavalier Paperbacks 1995
Warminster, Wiltshire BA12 OYD

Cover illustration by Joan Lampkin

ISBN 1-899470-10-7

Typeset by John Leighton Designs
Printed by Guernsey Press Co Ltd

CONTENTS

CHAPTER ONE   Hannah's ghost dog   1

CHAPTER TWO   On the trail of the mystery dog   11

CHAPTER THREE   Island campers   19

CHAPTER FOUR   What the dog thought   29

CHAPTER FIVE   Lonely dog of the island   37

CHAPTER SIX   Sam's plan   44

CHAPTER SEVEN   Skipper makes friends   49

CHAPTER EIGHT   Adventures with Skipper   57

CHAPTER NINE   Skipper is claimed   64

CHAPTER TEN   The Applebys tricked   72

CHAPTER ELEVEN   Skipper stolen   81

CHAPTER TWELVE   'Skipper – come home!'   85

CHAPTER THIRTEEN   Laddie needs the vet   90

CHAPTER FOURTEEN   A dog's disgrace   94

CHAPTER FIFTEEN   Hide-away!   97

CHAPTER SIXTEEN   Skipper to the rescue!   102

CHAPTER ONE
HANNAH'S GHOST DOG

The dog – there it was again!

No longer sleepy, Hannah Appleby heard nimble paws crunching the gravel outside. She moved softly across the bedroom and peered out of the open window.

Yes, it was a dog, sure enough, who padded across the drive and who was now stalking through the moonlit orchard. No one could possibly mistake him for a fox. She could see him clearly. He was a white Alsatian, and his coat gleamed wetly as though he had just been swimming in the sea. Hannah wanted to watch longer, but if she did not hurry to warn James, Alice and Sam they would not see the dog and then they would never believe he was a real one.

She ran across the room, out of the door and into Alice's bedroom, clicking on the light.

"Alice, wake up!" She shook her sister's shoulder. "It's the white dog again."

Alice shrugged off Hannah's hand, blinked and then buried her head in the pillow.

"Go back to bed," she said sleepily. "You've been dreaming."

"I haven't," Hannah denied. "The dog's in the orchard now. Come and see for yourself."

"Oh well" – Alice sat up resignedly and felt for her slippers – "I suppose I'd better come and put an end to this nonsense once and for all."

"You'll soon see it's not nonsense." Hannah broke off in impatience as Alice slowly put on her slippers, yawned, stretched her arms and reached for her dressing gown from the hook on the door. "Oh, do hurry, Alice. You'll miss him."

"I'm coming."

Alice put her arms into the sleeves of her dressing gown and began to tie the belt.

"Well, hurry up," Hannah urged, half-way to the door. "I'm going to wake James."

"And all the household, too, by the noise you're making," sighed Alice.

Hannah ran into the boys' room.

"It's the white dog," she said into the sleeping James's ear. "He's in the orchard. Or at least he was - I'm hoping he's still there."

"Me too!" James groaned, getting up.

"You're great, James."

Hannah rushed back to her own room with James not far behind.

Alice was already at the window.

"Seen it?" Hannah asked eagerly.

"Course not," Alice said scornfully. "Because it isn't there." She turned to James and groaned:

"Hannah's been seeing phantom dogs again."

"This wasn't a phantom dog," Hannah declared. "He's real. Look for yourselves!"

She pushed impatiently to the window and peered out. They had all been too slow, she realised with disappointment. The Alsatian had gone again.

"Now look, Hannah," James spoke with big-brotherly firmness, "This has got to stop. Every night this week you've had us out of bed to see your ghost dog."

"I never said it was a ghost dog," Hannah pointed out. "It's a flesh-and-blood, white Alsatian."

"White Alsatian!" James laughed. "Of all the dogs you might have seen it had to be a white Alsatian – something ghostly! There isn't a white Alsatian within miles of here. I tell you, Hannah, you must have dreamed it."

"Laddie heard it," Hannah insisted. "He barked."

James shrugged.

"Well, if you're going to imagine wolf dogs every time Laddie barks in his sleep –"

"You'd better see a doctor!" ended Alice.

Hannah sighed. It was maddening to have a brother and sister who – just because they were a year or two older than she was – seemed to have lost all sense of adventure.

Well, she must get proof about the dog. She looked out of the window. Drops of water glistened on the white roses. Rain had fallen. That meant there would be paw-prints on the softened ground, and paw-prints might lead her – where? "I'm the only one who's even seen him," Hannah comforted herself as she snuggled between the sheets. "And somehow that makes him my dog – my mystery dog!"

Hannah was wakened by the crowing of the

roosters. It was not quite light but she forced herself not to go to sleep again. If she did drop off, Frank, the cowman, would unloose Laddie and the paw prints would be confused. Hannah dressed and went downstairs, helping herself to a hunk of bread and butter from the pile on the kitchen dresser that had been placed there ready for her father and the men to have a snack before starting the early morning farm work.

Munching appreciatively – bread and butter had never before tasted so appetizing! – Hannah drew back the bolts and let herself out, trying to stifle her yawns. Laddie rattled his chain as he came out of his kennel to greet her, hoping for a scamper.

"Sorry, Laddie," Hannah said sympathetically as she patted the black-and-white sheepdog. "This is one time I can't take you. You'd run ahead and your paw-prints might put me on the wrong track."

As Hannah walked across the yard, a grey tabby cat stalked through the cat-run at the bottom of the harness room door. It was followed by four sleepy kittens.

"Sorry, pussies," Hannah told them. "I've wakened you too soon. You'll have to wait for the milking before you get your breakfast."

She pushed open the wicket gate and went into the orchard. The long wet grass was flattened, showing a track which led from the hole in the hedge towards the hen houses.

"I'm sure the dog can't be a poultry thief,"

4

Hannah told herself, "even though he may be hungry. Perhaps he prowls round the hen houses after mash and scraps."

She hurried towards the wire-netting of the chicken run. Yes, there on the muddy ground were a dog's paw-prints. She could see them plainly. They led to the feeding trough; and the trough had been licked quite clean. So the white Alsatian had come to the farm for food. Poor dog! He must have been hungry. Perhaps he was a stray. But where did he come from? Didn't he have an owner? Was he lost?

Hannah was mystified as she showed the tracks to her elder brother and sister when they came to see why she was out-of-doors before breakfast. But they were not impressed with what they saw.

"These tracks probably belong to some dog from the village," James said sceptically.

"Or a fox," put in Alice. "Yes, it might be a fox, prowling round the poultry pens. I'll warn Dad."

"There's no need to warn anyone," Hannah said impatiently. "It was the white Alsatian I saw last night. You can see him, too, if only you'll come and help me track him."

At that Sam, the youngest Appleby, popped his curly ginger head round the door.

"Hey, are you going tracking?" he asked eagerly. "Can I come?"

Hannah glanced from Sam to James and Alice, and decided it was no use trying to revive the older Applebys' lost sense of adventure. Well, there was always Sam – and he, at least, was enthusiastic.

"Very well, Sam," she agreed, smiling at her young brother. "Come on. Oh, and bring Darkie."

"Oh great!" Sam was thrilled. He scampered across the yard to get the saddle and bridle for his Shetland. I'll be ready in a minute."

Hannah did not bother about a saddle. She was too keen to get on the trail. With a sieve of oats she enticed Dapple from the corner of the paddock where the mare was grazing. She slipped the snaffle into Dapple's mouth, mounted and rode round the orchard hedge. By the time Sam trotted up on his tubby Shetland, Hannah was gazing at a new set of prints in the mud by the drinking trough.

"Look!" Hannah called, pointing with her stick to the trail of paw-marks. "They go towards the bridge over the field drain."

"Then let's follow them," whooped Sam.

Sam wasn't the only one who was keen. It was as much as Hannah could do to hold back Dapple to keep pace with Darkie's short strides. Dapple was full of the joy of the summer morning – fit and very fresh. When Hannah reined her up she gave a playful buck. Darkie, coming up behind, stopped short, pitching Sam on to his neck. "Hey," Sam protested, struggling back into the saddle. "You might give me warning, Hannah."

Hannah chuckled. "Sorry, Sam." She jerked her head sideways. "What do you make of that?"

Sam gazed at the paw-prints along the edge of the

ditch.

"I don't know," he admitted at last.

"This ditch leads into the stream at the end of the meadow," Hannah told him. "The dog seems to have been following the water."

"Perhaps he was thirsty," said Sam.

Hannah nodded and kicked Dapple to a gallop that left Sam bumping helplessly behind on Darkie's saddle.

The tracks led along the stream, down the meadow, past the fir copse until the two children came in sight of the sea. Hannah pulled up. The paw-prints had stopped on the beach.

She glanced to the cliffs at each side of the sandy bay, past the farthest point of the headland towards Bird Island. She dismounted and went forward, leading Dapple to the smugglers' path, the track which zigzagged down the cliff to the cove. Although the incoming tide had obviously washed away some paw-prints, Hannah could see some plainly marked in the sand which the waves had not yet reached.

She called to Sam: "The dog's paw-prints start again on the beach."

"Then let's go down." Sam jumped from his pony and ran, leading Darkie, towards the cliff path.

"It's no good," Hannah told him as he caught up with her.

"See!" she pointed to the sand below. "The tide's almost in. The prints will be covered in a few

7

minutes."

"They lead right along the beach and then disappear in the incoming tide," Sam mused. "I wonder where the dog was going."

"We shall never know," Hannah said sadly. "We'll just have to hope he comes back to the farm and that we'll have better luck tracking him next time."

Sam's face looked downcast. Then he brightened.

"Breakfast time," he announced as the chimes reached them from the clock on a distant church tower. "Tell you what, Hannah. I'll race you back to the farm."

She nodded to accept her brother's challenge. "The white dog's paw-prints do lead to the sea's edge," she was puzzling to herself. "And - oh yes! - every time I've seen the dog at night he's been wet as though he's been swimming the sea. I wonder if instead of trotting any farther along the beach this morning, he swam into the sea -"

She gazed towards Bird Island, a green and rocky paradise set not far off shore, in the deep blue sea. A strong dog like the Alsatian could easily swim that far.

"Ready, Hannah!" Sam turned round in the saddle twenty yards ahead of her.

Despite the good start that Hannah had given Sam, Dapple could not be held now that her head was towards home, and she soon flashed past the gallantly blowing Shetland. They were back in the paddock, Dapple's bridle was off and the mare was being rewarded with a slice of carrot when Darkie cantered up, snorting and puffing and looking pleased with himself at having been included in a race with one of the bigger ponies.

Barking excitedly, Laddie bounded to meet them. He was followed by Alice and James, on their way to visit the Shire foal in the field beyond the orchard.

"Well, have you seen your ghost dog?" Alice hailed.

"No, but we tracked him to the beach," said Sam.

"And then the tide covered his tracks," Hannah explained. "But I'm not beaten. The dog might come back tonight."

"Well, you won't hear him if he does," James said determinedly. "It's Laddie's bark that wakens you, isn't it, Hannah? Very well, I'll move his kennel to the other side of the house. Then you can't be wakened by him."

"Oh James!" Hannah groaned. "Don't do that – not when I'm so near finding out where the Alsatian comes from. I've already got a theory. Please!"

"It's for your own good, Hannah," Alice said with an expression of sorely tried patience. "We don't want to be stuffy, but you are being fanciful, you know."

"Rubbish!" retorted Hannah.

That night when Hannah's steady breathing made the patchwork quilt rise and fall as she slept, Laddie stirred in his kennel, put his head outside and gave a bark.

"What was that?" On the other side of the house James jerked awake and asked himself the question.

As though in reply, Laddie barked again.

The sheepdog was barking in his sleep, decided James. Yet somehow he sounded wideawake. James got out of bed and ran to the window. Next moment he held his breath as he saw in the moonlight a white Alsatian, steadily licking up the leavings of mash in the chicken trough – and Laddie, whose job it was to show intruders that they were unwelcome, was sitting outside his kennel, wagging approval at the midnight visitor!

"Gosh!" gasped James. "So Hannah was right after all. A white Alsatian who only comes out at night – a real mystery dog!"

CHAPTER TWO

ON THE TRAIL OF THE MYSTERY DOG

"Hannah!" James shook his sister, whispering urgently. "Wake up!"

Hannah stirred and sighed. "Go away. It's not time to get up."

"The mystery dog!" James said in her ear, and Hannah saw that even James was excited about the Alsatian. "You were right. I've just seen him."

She pushed back the bedclothes and sprang out, fully dressed. James blinked as she grabbed for her shoes.

"So – you went to bed with your clothes on, Hannah!" he gasped.

"All except my shoes. I meant to keep awake to see the dog," Hannah explained. "But I must have dropped off. I was so tired after watching for him all those other nights."

"Never mind about that now." James was halfway to the door. "Hurry. I've called Alice and we're all set to solve the mystery of your white Alsatian."

The three children tiptoed downstairs and crept out of the house. Hannah's spirits soared. At last the older ones believed her.

"Ssh!" James warned as Alice's foot crunched on the gravel of the drive. "Keep to the grass. I think the dog's still around the farm."

The trio moved stealthily towards the moonlit orchard and suddenly they saw a sleek white shape moving between the apple trees.

"There!" Hannah gripped Alice's arm and pointed triumphantly. "See?"

The dog heard her. His ears twitched. Next minute he had gone, bounding over the long grass and through the hedge to the meadow. James broke into a run.

"Follow him."

"We'll never keep up on foot." Hannah made for the paddock. "Let's get the ponies." Dapple, who sensed Hannah's mood and was always eager for an outing, was easily caught, but Alice's dun pony, Prince, played up, dodging his mistress and cantering to the other end of the paddock.

"Leave him," called Hannah as Prince evaded Alice for the third time. She leaned down from Dapple's back and stretched out a hand to her sister. "Come up with me. Dapple can carry us both."

Meanwhile James had pressed one of the Shire horses into service. From the height of Captain's seventeen hands he was leading the field at a startled gallop.

"There he goes!" Alice cried suddenly, and pointed excitedly towards the fir copse round which the white Alsatian was running.

"That must be his usual route," said Hannah. "It's the way his tracks led this morning."

Captain and Dapple thundered after the dog. Their riders halted them at the edge of the cliff and James peered over. The white Alsatian was leaving the smuggler's path and cutting across the beach at a steady lope.

Hannah gazed as the dog waded into the sea. Soon he began to swim powerfully towards Bird Island.

"Just as I thought," said Hannah. "So that's where he hides up during the day." Spell-bound, she watched the Alsatian swim strongly to the cove that lay between the rocks on Bird Island. "I vote we lay the lobster pots after breakfast; then we can scout round for the dog's hide-out."

"Good idea, Hannah," voted James.

James was down at the beach early in the morning, baiting the lobster pots, while the two girls raided the biscuit tin and begged the remains of yesterday's stew from their mother to make the Alsatian a tasty meal.

Sam accompanied them as they dragged the dinghy over the sand to the water's edge. Because he weighed the lightest, the youngest Appleby sat in the boat at the tiller while Alice, Hannah and James, waded, pushing the dinghy into deep water.

"She's afloat," James called to the girls, leaping aboard. "Don't get left behind."

"Not likely!" Alice said, expertly scrambling into the boat after him. "Wait for me!" Hannah begged, nearly getting a soaking but managing to haul herself inboard just in time.

James hoisted the lug sail and the wind caught the boat, swinging her out to sea. He went to the tiller and took over from Sam. A look of content settled on the older boy's face as he set course for Bird Island. James loved the sea and was never happier than when he was aboard the Curlew.

"We'll go round the Lion's Head and drop the lobster pots," he said. "Then we'll be free to look for the dog."

A freshening breeze met them as they rounded the headland and entered the narrow sound. James's blissful expression changed to one of anxiety. Hannah and Alice looked at each other as they knew James's sea-sick symptoms.

"Shall I take over?" Hannah asked sympathetically, moving towards the tiller.

"No thanks." James attempted a joke: "I'd rather risk death from sea-sickness than shipwreck. Anyhow, I've got to get used to it if I'm going to sea when I'm sixteen."

James stuck to his post. The craggy point of Bird Island loomed nearer. James sailed as close to the rocks as he could. Then he gave the order to drop the lobster pots. The wicker cages disappeared one after the other. Only the bobbing floats remained to show where they were.

"Now for the dog," said James with undisguised excitement as he put the Curlew about and made for Bird Island's only beach, trying to forget about his queasy tummy.

Soon the four children were clambering ashore. They beached the boat and hurried up the path towards the middle of the island with Hannah carrying the dog's meal in an enamel bowl.

"Good dog!"

"Here, boy!"

Alice and Hannah began to call and James and Sam whistled. But no answering bark betrayed the whereabouts of the white Alsatian. The only sounds were the gurgle and splash of the sea against the rocks, the shrieks of the herring gulls and the lonely clanging of the bell buoy at the entrance to the sound.

Hannah tightly held the food bowl, trying not to spill any of the contents as she scrambled up the island track. At last the children reached the grassy slopes of the island and looked around. Short turf stretched for about a quarter of a mile in either direction. From it steep cliffs dropped to the sea, except where there were coves or inlets. There was no sign of any four-footed life. Puffins, guillemots, razor-bills and gulls there were - in their thousands. But no white Alsatian.

He had completely disappeared.

"Where is he?" pondered Hannah. "He must be somewhere because we saw him swim across."

"Why he should live here at all beats me," said Alice. "There are no rabbits for food, and no fresh water, and I'm quite sure he can't catch the birds."

James nodded. "Let's spread out," he suggested. "We could search the top of the island. Then from the cliffs we ought to be able to see if the dog's anywhere below. Alice, take Sam with you, but be careful that he doesn't go near the edge."

Sam grimaced. He did not like to be reminded that he was the youngest Appleby. But if that was the price he had to pay to be included in the older ones' adventures he was prepared to accept it. So his frown melted to a good-natured grin.

The Applebys fanned out, peering into gullies and over cliffs, and exploring all beaches and inlets.

Suddenly Hannah stopped. Just above the high-water mark in a small cove she caught sight of the keel of an upturned boat. Leading to it, in the sand, were many paw-prints.

"Hey, come and look at this!" Hannah shouted.

"It looks like a yacht's tender," James panted, out of breath with running, "or it might be a trawler's lifeboat. It's quite small. Perhaps it was washed off some boat in a storm, and it was cast up here during a high tide."

"But the paw-prints!" Hannah insisted. "What about them?" At that moment a sharp, short bark sounded from under the boat.

"The Alsatian!" Sam whispered excitedly, gripping James's arm. "He must be using the boat as a sort of kennel."

The dog barked again, fiercely this time.

"And he's making it clear he doesn't want us to go near it," said James.

"All the same, I'm going to try," decided Hannah, holding the bowl in front of her and tiptoeing towards the keel-uppermost boat. "Good dog!" she coaxed. "Come and have some stew." A white muzzle showed from under the boat and a growl rumbled out.

" He doesn't trust us," said Sam.

"Why not leave the food and go away?" suggested Alice.

"Oh, let's try once more," Hannah pleaded.

She took a specially tempting-looking piece of meat from the stew in the bowl and threw it towards the upturned boat.

"Good shot, Hannah!" Sam exclaimed excitedly as the lump of meat fell near the Alsatian's jaws.

But the dog was not as pleased as Hannah had expected.

"Grrrr!" he growled.

"Now we have upset him!" Alice sighed. "Oh dear! He just won't trust us – and he does look such a wonderful dog."

"I expect he's been living on his own for some time," James speculated. "He won't be used to people, and so he's bound to be on his guard at first."

"We'll have to get him used to us gradually," said Alice.

"But how can we?" Hannah asked. "We're always in bed when he comes to the mainland."

James looked thoughtful.

"Yes, I see what you mean," he nodded. "But suppose we camped out on the island, fairly near to the Alsatian's boat. Then he'd soon be used to having us around all the time."

"Now that," voted Hannah approvingly, thumping her big brother on his back, "is an idea that shows sheer genius."

CHAPTER THREE
ISLAND CAMPERS

After the farmhouse tea, the Applebys told their Mum and Dad about the mysterious white dog who visited the farm by night and lived by day on Bird Island.

"He sounds like a castaway," Mrs Appleby decided. "Poor thing! It must be dreadful for a dog to be homeless."

"Yes, that's the whole point," Hannah agreed. "I knew you'd understand, Mum. But you see we can't give him a home because he won't let us. We've got to make him trust us first. James's had a simply wonderful idea about how we might go about it."

James explained in detail about the camping plan.

"I don't know." Mrs Appleby looked anxious. "I don't like the thought of you all spending the night alone on the island."

"But need we be alone?" Alice suggested. "Couldn't Dad come over to sleep – as he used to when we first started to camp in the field?"

"Yes, that's an idea," Mr Appleby mused, remembering all the happy days he had spent under canvas when he was a boy. "I've often thought Bird Island would make a good camping spot."

"Oh, Dad, you're the best dad in the world." Hannah gave him a big hug. "And everything's much more fun when you join in."

"Yes, Dad," Sam said wholeheartedly. "You're

always able to show us the right way to do things."

"Well, I'll only be able to sleep in the island camp," Mr Appleby pointed out. "I shall have to get back early in the morning for milking."

"I'll ferry you back in the dinghy soon after dawn," James offered, "and I'll pick you up every evening."

"In time for camp supper," Alice put in. "I want you to try some of my cheese dreams, Dad."

"Fair enough, Alice," Mr Appleby laughed. "So long as the dreams can't turn into nightmares."

"When can we go?" Sam asked excitedly. "Now?"

"Not tonight, Sam," Mr Appleby said. "There's a lot to do. We'll have to get the provisions across, including water. There's no fresh water on Bird Island."

"We could sail the water bin across in the boat," James suggested. "Then we'll need firewood and the cooking things, and of course the tents."

"And dog biscuits," Hannah added. "A drinking bowl –" She broke off suddenly. "If there isn't any water on the island – wherever does the poor dog get a drink from?"

"He comes across to the mainland for food and drink," James said. "And I bet he's often thirsty as well as hungry."

"Well he won't need to be any more," said Hannah. "He'll have his own nice clean bowl not far from his boat-home and lots of good camp food!"

Sam looked meaningly at the grandfather clock that was ticking away the seconds.

"Roll on tomorrow," he murmured and his eyes were shining with excitement.

Next day Mr Appleby helped James, Hannah and Sam to load the tents, ground sheets, bedding and cooking equipment into a large wheelbarrow while Mrs Appleby and Alice were making out a camp menu and packing up provisions.

At last, they set off across the fields to the cliff top. There they had to unload and carry the camping kit down the smugglers's path to the cove.

While the others waited impatiently on the rocks, Mr Appleby and James ferried the tents and stores across. There was not enough room for the provisions and all the Applebys.

When James and his father came back they carefully carried the water aboard.

"Well, that's that!" Mr Appleby decided after a last minute inspection. "I'll have to leave you youngsters now. I've got a lot to do around the farm this morning."

"That's all right, Dad," James assured him. "We can cope."

"I'm sure you can," Mr Appleby told him. "All the same, I'll take a walk down here after lunch and have a look at you through the binoculars, just to see how you're getting on."

"And I'll be across to pick you up tonight at eight, Dad," James arranged. "We'll rig your tent and have everything ready for you."

Mr Appleby, always a keen camper when a boy, hummed a happy tune as he left. He was pleased that his children wanted him to share their healthy, outdoor activities, and also, being a dog lover, he was as eager as they were that the Alsatian should be won over by kindness. He turned to wave at his children before he went out of sight.

James answered the hail as he hoisted sail, and cast off. The sails filled, but when they were just off the point, the wind dropped.

James groaned as he lowered the sails, and shipped the oars.

But even though they all rowed, they made slow progress. The dinghy was heavily laden and the flood tide was against them.

At last, hot and out of breath, they reached the beach. James slipped off his trainers and jumped into the shallow wavelets to guide the dinghy ashore.

"Steady, now," he warned Hannah who was standing up to follow him. "Keep the boat trimmed. Nobody move until she's beached. We mustn't upset the water bin."

At last the keel touched firm sand.

"Oh look!" While wading ashore Alice pointed to the rocks beyond the beach. "There he is!"

Looking dazzlingly white against the blue sky the Alsatian was standing on a big rock, ears at the alert, keen gaze fixed on the landing party.

"Oh, I do hope he doesn't think we're his

enemies," Hannah said feelingly.

"Gosh! I've never seen a more super-looking dog!" exclaimed Sam. "I know he'll want to be friends with me!"

"Now he's turning his head on one side, as though he's puzzled," decided Alice, shielding her eyes with a hand to get a better view. "And he seems as though he might be a bit angry. Oh, if only we knew what he was thinking. Then we might know better how to set about making friends with him."

Paws placed firmly on the rock above them, the Alsatian craned his head to watch them. Why were they coming here? He wanted to bark, and tell them to go away. But though the bark quivered in his throat, he held it back.

Instead a whimper tore at his heart. He did not know why. All he knew was that the children on the beach reminded him of a happier time in his life before he had lost his master and his master's family.

In those days he had been given all the love that a dog needs. Kind hands had stroked him. He had been fed every day. Cool water had been put out for him to lap when he had been thirsty. There had been a master whom he loved and tried to please, so that he could hear master say 'Good dog,' and know that he had earned the praise.

Sometimes he had known the loving arms of young human beings round his neck, hugging him. And several times there had been a young boy with whom he had romped.

23

And now here were other human children. Dare he make friends with them? He longed to run to greet them, wagging his tail, putting his paws on the shoulder of the bigger boy, and licking his cheek – then rolling over and having a rough and tumble with the younger boy, so that he might believe that the good days had returned.

But perhaps it would not be like that. Perhaps they did not really like dogs. Suppose they wanted to make him a prisoner or do him some harm? Could they have come to the island to drive him away?

Things had happened to him since he had got lost – things which had lessened his faith in many human beings, but he did not like to think about that.

Suddenly, despite the heat of the sun, he felt cold and lonely, and because the children reminded him so heart-breakingly of his former life he felt even more alone. Whimpering to himself, he slunk towards some boulders to hide, but though he put his head on his outstretched front paws he did not snooze. He lay there, waiting, on the alert, so that he might be ready to act, if those who might be his enemies ventured too near.

Down below on the beach, Sam turned to help the others to carry the kit ashore.

"The Alsatian's gone now," he declared, "but I bet anything you like he'll be trotting down to the beach to see what's going on."

Meanwhile James was trying to decide where to pitch camp. He looked at the old overturned boat that the mystery dog used as his kennel.

"We mustn't be far away from the dog," he decided. Then he pointed to a grassy patch beyond the beach where some bushes might act as a windbreak for the tents. "We'll pitch there."

It was not until they started to put up the tents, that they noticed a stiffish breeze which would have been welcome a little earlier in the dinghy's sails, but which now made the tent canvas difficult to handle.

James capably took charge, and stationed Alice, Hannah and Sam on the windward side of the tents to hold down the canvas while he knocked in the pegs.

They were too busy to notice the dog crouching on the soft turf some twenty yards away, watching them.

In utter mystification, head on one side, the dog gazed at them.

After he had hidden behind the boulders, he had waited, on his guard, for them to approach. But when they had not bothered with him, he had grown bolder. Perhaps they were not going to chase him away after all.

Then he had heard their voices and the noise of the pegs knocked into the ground, and the flapping of the tents in the wind. Curiosity had become too much for him. Human beings often did things that were puzzling to dogs, but, in all his adventures, this was the most puzzling thing that had ever happened. What in the world were they doing?

Not realising that the dog was so near, the Applebys stared in dismay at the tent which had now blown adrift on a thorn bush. A sudden gust of wind had carried the canvas away before they had been able to peg it, and now it was out of reach on a high thorn bush.

"I could kick myself!" Sam exclaimed feelingly. "If only I hadn't let go of the canvas."

"Cheer up, Sam," Alice patted her younger brother's shoulder in a big-sisterly way. "The Applebys never admit defeat. We're not beaten yet."

"I should say not," James agreed.

Sam, to make amends, scampered to the boat, and came back carrying the boat hook.

"Thanks, Sam," said James as his young brother handed it to him.

"Got it!" The eldest Appleby shouted in triumph when the boat-hook caught in the folds of the tent and brought it within reach. "Careful, everybody. Steady as you go. Don't tug too hard."

At last they brought the tent to earth, and weighted it down with a rock.

"Cheers!" whooped Hannah. "That's saved the day."

"I vote we leave putting it up until after lunch," proposed Sam. "I'm famished."

Soon curls of blue smoke were rising from the wood fire and Alice was stirring the contents of a saucepan the outside of which was black from many camp fires. Appetizing smells filled the air.

Sam sniffed ecstatically.

"It smells even better out-of-doors than when Mother's cooking in the kitchen at home," he declared. "Gosh! If the dog gets a whiff of this I should think even he will have to come and investigate."

Sure enough they saw the Alsatian's white head peering round a rock.

"Come on, old chap!" Sam called. "Come and have some stew!"

At the sound of the boy's voice the Alsatian's ears dropped. He looked round warily and a low-throated growl came from his mouth.

"Don't be angry," pleaded Sam. "We want to be friends."

The Alsatian glanced up the cliff, saw Sam and retreated, tail between his legs to crawl under the boat. He growled warningly.

"Now you've scared him," Hannah told Sam disappointedly as she came up to see what was happening. "You've undone all the good work. The smell of food was just tempting him out and you had to rush him. It may be hours before he ventures out again."

James endorsed Hannah's words as she and Sam returned to the camp-fire.

"We mustn't try to force ourselves on the dog," he said.

"We must just carry on as if he wasn't there. I know it's hard. I'm longing to go and have a look at him, but it would only make him more on his guard."

"I'm sorry," said Sam. "But I could see he wanted some food and I thought if I just encouraged him he'd come to me."

"Never mind," said Hannah. "It can't be helped now. You'll know better next time."

Then she realised she was being bossy, so she did not say any more. Instead she cut a hunk of bread from the loaf and passed her plate to Alice to receive a generous ladleful of Irish stew.

"Leave some for the dog," she reminded her sister. "We'll put it out for him when it's gone cold."

After the meal was over, Alice fetched a bucketful of sea water in which to wash up the plates and knives and forks. Then she and Hannah mixed the remains of the Irish stew and a round of bread. They put it into an enamel dish and carried it down to the rocks.

"We'll leave it just here." Hannah chose a spot out of sight of the camp and well within scent-wafting distance of the Alsatian's hide-out. "Perhaps he'll come and eat it when we've gone away. If one thing's more likely than another to make him want to be friends, it's our cooking!"

CHAPTER FOUR
WHAT THE DOG THOUGHT

"Do you remember the food that I put out for the Alsatian?" Hannah excitedly asked a few hours later. "Well, it's gone!"

"Hurrah!" Sam exclaimed. "Soon he'll be sitting down by our camp fire, waiting for scraps."

"Yes, won't Dad be pleased?" James happened at that moment to look towards the sun which was already low in the western sky and then consulted his watch. "Gosh! It's time to fetch him. Coming, Hannah?"

"I'll help Alice with the supper," Hannah decided. "Take Sam."

As the two boys were sailing to the mainland, Hannah and Alice lit the fire, put slices of cheese between two thick pieces of bread and butter and skewered the pieces together ready to toast over the fire.

Hannah scrambled on to a rock which made an excellent look-out.

"Start toasting!" she shouted to her sister a little later. "They're just sailing into the cove."

Soon Mr Appleby, James and Sam were sampling the toasted 'cheese dreams' and finding them delicious. Dusk fell as they sat round the dying fire.

Hannah stifled a yawn, and hoped her father had not seen it because he would be sure to decide it was bed-time if he knew she was sleepy.

While the others chatted about the camp and the white Alsatian, Hannah's eyelids felt heavy. There! She had yawned before she had realised it.

"Bed-time, children!" Mr Appleby decided, and firmly but good-naturedly dealt with the cries of protest.

Soon Hannah crawled into her sleeping-bag beside Alice in the girls' ridge-tent.

What was that? Hannah sat upright, suddenly wideawake. It seemed only a moment since she had snuggled down in her sleeping bag. But it was really four hours ago.

She sat listening. What had wakened her? Was it the dog? Her heart leapt as she heard a snuffling noise.

Trying to control her excitement, Hannah wriggled out of her sleeping bag and crawled towards the flap of the tent.

Peeping out she saw the dog in the moonlight. Feeling sure that everyone was sound asleep, he was – with doggy inquisitiveness – inspecting the camp site. The washing-up water bucket caught his eye. He went to it, bent his head to drink, found that the water was salty and moved away to the water bowl that James had put near the dog's old boat 'kennel'.

Hannah crawled to the pile of her clothes on the ground sheet at the foot of her sleeping bag and felt in the pocket of her shorts for the dog biscuit she had carried all yesterday – just in case. Stealthily she crept back to the tent opening and threw out the biscuit.

The dog stood quite still, some distance away – half-way to his boat kennel. Hannah could see his eyes glowing through the dim light. Then he turned his head away, and dropped his nose to the ground again. He soon found the biscuit, and his handsome face wrinkled up in pleasure – almost like a smile – as the biscuit made a delightful 'crunchy' noise between his strong teeth.

Hannah watched him padding round the site for a while before, shivering now, she wriggled back into her sleeping bag and snuggled down.

When she opened her eyes again she was dazzled by the morning sunlight that slanted through the open tent flap.

"Wake up, sleepy-heads!" Mr Appleby urged the two girls.

Hannah scrambled into her clothes. When she was helping to get the breakfast, she told them what she had seen.

"And he never even knew I was watching him," she ended.

"Good!" Mr Appleby exclaimed. "Don't take any notice of him – not even if he comes quite near to you. He's got to find out all about us – and get used to our smell! – before he'll trust us." He broke off to look at the sky. "Be prepared for rain today – maybe thunder, too."

"Aye, aye, Dad!"

James sailed his father across to the mainland. Then all that morning while the children bathed, played rounders on the beach, and tidied up the camp site, they tried hard to forget that the Alsatian was snoozing in his boat kennel. But it was during the midday meal that they found they could not completely ignore the dog any longer.

"Don't look round now," Hannah whispered, fork poised as she was about to spear a sausage. "I think we're being watched."

"Have you only just realised that?" James retorted in an undertone. "I've known it for some time."

"Yes," Sam added softly, I heard him having a good lap of water a few moments ago."

"It's the sultry weather making him thirsty," put in Alice. "The poor dog's feeling the heat." She fanned herself with a saucepan lid. "So am I."

"Me for another bathe this afternoon," voted Hannah.

"If you don't get wet enough without going in the water," said Sam, looking up at a storm cloud on the horizon. "I smell rain."

Hannah munched absent-mindedly. "What's the dog doing now?" she asked. "Can anyone see him without turning round?"

"I can see something white reflected in the shiny part of the new saucepan," Alice said. "He seems to be coming nearer. He's by the thorn bush now."

Hannah jabbed another deliciously browned sausage.

"Hungry though I am," she affirmed, "I'd gladly give the dog half my lunch if only he'd join us."

"Me too," said James. "But we've still got to go on taking no notice of him. Dad was right –"

He broke off to listen. All of them stopped breathing. Cautious paws crunched on the shingle. The dog was slowly coming towards them.

Sam held himself tensely. How he longed to look round!

"Just go on behaving normally," James said in a hoarse, excited voice. "If we stop talking he might get suspicious."

"Lovely weather we're having for this time of the year," Hannah improvised without thought. "I mean apart from the thunder that's in the air –"

She stopped talking. From a few yards behind them – quite near, the children had heard the dog give a short bark. It had a friendly note, and it seemed to say: "Here's me." They exchanged glances. Was the dog puzzled and hurt because they had ignored him? "Woof – Woof-woof!"

"I said: 'Here's me!' – Gosh – that's what the dog seemed to say as plain as anything, Sam decided and, unable to do otherwise, turned round. But it did not matter. All the others had done the same.

"Gosh!" exclaimed James softly, echoing all their thoughts. "Just look at him!"

They were spell-bound by the beauty of the snowy-white Alsatian. There was something quite breath-taking about his lean grace, and the sleek outline of his head, with his ears pricked and keen, as he stood motionless on the shingle, showing himself so that they might admire him and be friendly.

"Good dog!" murmured Alice, overcome with affection for him. "Oh, good dog."

Slowly the tail began to wag. Long, long ago he had heard the word good. It was a word that he had been taught when he was a puppy, and it meant that human beings were pleased with him – that they liked him.

While these human children had been on the island, they had given him cool, clear water, and food that was tastier than he had known for a long time. Now they had said he was 'good.' He was certainly a very happy Alsatian indeed.

Ah! Now he seemed to remember that after the word good had been spoken he was sometimes rewarded by being given a titbit.

But sometimes, in the old days before he got lost, the reward was forgotten. Then he had to remind the humans. He remembered now – a way that nearly always earned him a titbit.

He padded to a firm part of the shingle, sat down, reared up, and with his front paws neatly held before him, he pleaded for a reward.

"He's begging!" Hannah breathed. "Oh, isn't he wonderful? Have you ever seen such a simply fantastic dog?"

Alice already had a sausage between her finger and thumb to throw.

"Don't!" Sam cautioned, grabbing Alice's wrist. "Let me take him this on a plate. I'm smaller than any of you, and he's less likely to be scared of me."

Sam, Hannah and Alice all dragged their gazes away from the dog to look inquiringly at James. "Very well," James said at last. "Good luck, Sam, old son."

Aware of the hopes they were pinning on him, and keen not to let them down, Sam gripped the enamelled tin plate on which were left two and a half sausages. Step by step the youngest Appleby moved towards the begging Alsatian. The dog's friendly brown eyes were fixed on the boy, watching him. His black nose twitched as he smelt the food. Drops of saliva formed along his lower jaw.

"Good boy!" Sam murmured, going nearer, plate held out in front of him.

This was brilliant!

Sam's thoughts were triumphant. Gosh! Within a few moments, the dog would be eating out of his hand. He would be won over! How pleased Dad would be when they told him! What a thrill when Dad came to the island camp that evening, and found that the Alsatian was one of the family.

"There's a nice fellow," Sam encouraged, while the others waited, hardly daring to breathe, and the mystery dog swayed slightly in his begging position, as though he longed to drop on to four paws to run and greet the young boy.

But the dog knew that he must keep begging if he was to earn titbits that were being brought to him.

Joy surged in his heart. At last! Here were human beings whom he could trust.

As though spell-bound Sam kept his eyes on the dog, and that's why he did not notice the slippery piece of seaweed that lay across a smooth, sea washed stone half-embedded on the shingle.

"Look out!" Hannah urged – too late!

CHAPTER FIVE

LONELY DOG OF THE ISLAND

Sam's right foot came down on the seaweed and skidded off the rock. He fell forward towards the dog. The sausages were flung headlong and the tin plate, which Sam still tightly clutched even when he was falling, crashed against the dog's head.

"Sorry, old boy!" Sam gasped.

"Grrr-! Grrr!" growled the pained and angry Alsatian. So he was being made a fool of, thought the dog. And he'd so badly wanted to be friends. He backed away across the shingle. With outstretched hands, Sam tried to catch him.

"Oh you idiot!" exclaimed Hannah. "Why didn't you look where you were going?"

"Don't grab at the dog for goodness sake," shouted Alice. "That's making him more scared than ever."

"You've done enough harm, Sam," yelled James, jumping to his feet and running after the dog. "Leave him to me now."

The Alsatian's ears fell, and his tail drooped between his legs. He had been struck. Now they were shouting at him. They did not want him after all. They were enemies - not friends. The big boy was even chasing him.

"Hey, come back!" begged James. "Please come back!"

But in headlong flight, pausing only to bark

angrily when his old boat 'kennel' was in sight, the Alsatian bolted for cover.

As the children ran up they could hear the dog's steady panting from under the boat.

"I didn't mean to hit you, old boy," Sam said near the gap. "Please let's be friends now. Give me another chance."

"Grrr-!" answered the Alsatian.

"Here - try him with this," Hannah suggested, handing James a couple of sausages which she had picked up from the shingle.

James held the sausages to the gap. A black nose twitched towards it; then drew back.

"He won't be tempted," groaned Alice.

"Who can blame him when we're all talking at once?" James whispered. "Now let's sit down quietly and soon perhaps he'll realise we don't mean him any harm."

Angrily, the dog crouched under his boat while the children squatted down, hugging their knees as they waited. Grrr-! So they were not going away. They had trapped him in his own kennel, and were keeping him a prisoner there. Why had he trusted them?

Then he remembered that he had once trusted all human beings.

But that was before he somehow got lost ... He had had to forage for food, to hunt and to beg or steal. Whenever he had tipped up a dust-bin to get at the scraps inside, he had been chased away. Once an angry housewife had hit him across his rump with a broom.

Another time he had hung around a butcher's shop begging for titbits and a man had thrown a chopping board at him. It had fallen with a dreadful noise on the pavement just behind him.

Once he had wriggled through a gap in the fence of a poultry farm, searching for scraps of mash to fill his empty tummy. The poultry farmer had thought he was after his chickens and he had shot at him, and missed.

The mystery dog shivered again as he remembered it all. After several hungry days he had learned to hunt at night.

He had come to Bird Island, kennelled up during the day under the shipwrecked dinghy and visited Headland Farm at night to find food. He had lived quite comfortably on Laddie's leavings, on fowl mash and calf cake.

Then the children had invaded his island. But he had thought that at last he might have found what he most longed for – human friends. In his puzzled doggy brain he had even thought that they might take the place of his lost master. But he had been wrong. They made noises and threw things at him just as other people had done. Nobody wanted a stray dog. The Alsatian cowered. Would he always be homeless and unloved?

Meanwhile, outside the boat 'kennel', James glanced at the storm clouds.

"Ouch!" shivered Hannah as a large drop of rain slid down her neck. "It's started."

"We'd better leave the dog for a moment," James decided, "and get the gear under cover before everything's drenched."

Soon the rain was followed by thunder and lightning. The lightning soon passed, but the rain became torrential.

The children sat inside the tents and listened to the lashing of the rain on the taut canvas. Alice bumped her head against the roof and it began to leak.

"Draw your finger down from the leak to the edge of the tent," James suggested. "That's supposed to lead the rain away."

Alice tried, but somehow it did not seem to work. To make things more uncomfortable, rain had collected in a hollow near the stunted bushes and was trickling under the ground sheet.

A little distance away, the Alsatian lay in his boat 'kennel'. The rain beat loudly on the upturned keel. Those flashes and the rolls of thunder had made him tremble. Somehow he had connected them with the human children being angry with him.

Now – oh dear! – water was flooding into the only 'home' that he knew. He tried to stand up, but bumped his head on the boat seat. In dismay, he looked down at the water that was rising round his paws, and flowing to the other side of the kennel.

What was happening? What new calamity was this?

Agonisingly he howled.

Above the noise of the rain James heard the howl.

"That was the Alsatian!" he exclaimed, putting his head out of the tent and blinking into the streaming rain. "Golly! Look!"

Three other Appleby heads peered wetly out of the tent flap. Not far from the old boat 'kennel', rain was running in rivulets into a rocky pool which was overflowing in a stream that seeped under the Alsatian's 'kennel.'

The four children ran to the spot. Quickly James demonstrated what should be done. With the boat-hook he and Sam prised some rocks from the other side of the pool so that the water drained away to the sea down a gully in the shingle.

"Done it!" Sam declared breathlessly a few moments later, as they watched the water drain away from the upturned boat.

"We've turned the stream. It won't run under his kennel again."

"Grrr!" growled the dog, on the defensive, when he heard the noise of the heavy stones being moved.

"Ahoy there, youngsters!"

Four drenched figures, hair matted, and with their vision blurred by rain, turned to see their father in a borrowed motor-boat and wearing oilskins, dropping anchor in the cove.

"Are we glad to see you, Dad!" exclaimed James.

They rushed to tell him about how they had nearly won over the dog, and how Sam had had a mishap which had made the dog distrust them all.

"And to top it all," sighed Alice, "We're drenched to the skin, and a lot of the camp kit is soaked."

"This cloud-burst would swamp out almost any camp site," consoled Mr Appleby, feeling very sorry for his youngsters. "That's why I came for you. Pack up! We're going home as quickly as we can, so that you can have hot baths and dry your clothes."

"Oh must we, Dad?" wailed Hannah. "Couldn't we dry out our things in the sun?"

"You won't see much sun today, poppet," chuckled her father, "but you'll feel a lot more rain! Come aboard girls. There's some emergency chocolate in the locker. Tuck into it while I help the boys to load up the camp kit."

"And leave some chocolate for us," Sam called over his shoulder.

Before they chugged out of the cove, with the dinghy in tow behind the motor-boat, the children's gaze turned to the upturned boat. The rain glistened on the keel.

"So long, Island Dog!" Sam murmured. "We'll still put food and water for you in the farmyard as usual. So you won't go hungry."

Some moments later the lashing rain became only a shower. A rainbow made an arc above the island.

The Alsatian crept from under the upturned boat. He shook himself. Then he stretched, and sniffed the sea air. He cocked his head as he heard the sound of the Applebys' voices carried across the waves.

So the human children had gone. He sniffed round the camp site. Slowly he padded down the beach to where wavelets rippled over a sand bar.

Once more he had the island to himself. He tried to wag his tail. But instead it just drooped in dejection.

Overhead a herring gull wheeled, and cackled, taunting him.

Suddenly the island dog whimpered and felt lonelier than ever before.

CHAPTER SIX
SAM'S PLAN

"What now?" asked James as, in dry clothes, the Appleby children had tea in the farmhouse kitchen while their wet clothes dried out in front of the blazing fire in the open grate. "What do you think we ought to do about the Alsatian, Dad?"

"I'm every bit as fond of dogs as you are, and I want to do what's best for him," said Mr Appleby after a moment's thought, "but there are one or two things to be considered."

"Such as?" prompted Sam.

"Well," said Mr Appleby after a long drink of tea, "the dog's obviously been lost for some time. He's a fine, pedigree dog and he's proved that he isn't a sheep-worrier. So it isn't likely he's a dog who has been turned out because he's unwanted or got vicious habits."

"Anybody would be proud to own a dog like that one!" Hannah said staunchly.

Mr Appleby nodded. "You can be quite sure that the owner must be badly wanting him back."

"Yes, I would if he had belonged to me," agreed James.

"Gosh! I'd never stop searching if he'd been my dog and he'd got lost."

"And of course," Alice declared, "it's the duty of everyone who finds a lost dog to do everything to restore it to the owner."

"I'm glad you understand that," Mr Appleby said with a relieved sigh, "because I made a point of calling in at the police-station this morning and telling Sergeant Benson all about the dog. He's never heard of anyone around here losing a white Alsatian, but he's making inquiries at other police-stations, because the dog may have come some distance. You can be sure he'll do everything he can to find the owner."

"It's my theory the Alsatian was on some boat or other, and somehow went overboard," speculated James.

"That's possible," agreed their father. "Anyway, until the owner is found, Sergeant Benson has agreed to leave the dog in our custody, so to speak. He thinks that it's best to win him over by patience."

"And I had to ruin everything by treading on that seaweed!" groaned Sam.

"Never mind, Sam, old son," consoled James patting his younger brother on the back. "You'll do better next time."

Sam's eyes were shining. Already an idea as to how he might win over the dog was forming in his mind.

"You bet. I'll do better next time!" he exclaimed. "The dog was just longing to be pals and romp with me before I tripped up and the plate landed on his head."

That evening the rain cleared but a sea mist drifted over the coast, blotting out the headland and Bird Island.

Sam, cleaning out his pet rabbits in the loft, peered through the cobwebby window, and turned his gaze in the direction of the mist-hidden island.

"We'll soon be pals, Island Dog," he murmured, conjuring up in his mind's eye, the spell-binding vision of the dog as he had sat up and begged on the beach earlier that day. "And I'll be your friend until we find your own master."

But his plan must be kept secret – or the others would not let him go through with it.

Sam, full of hope, began to whistle.

For once, Sam was not late for supper.

"Can I go out for five minutes, Mum?" he casually asked, when he had eaten.

"What is it?" Hannah asked. "Forgotten to feed your rabbits?"

"No, Cotton-tail and Lop-ears have had their meal," Sam said. He tried to sound off-hand so as to put them on the wrong track. "It's something else I want to do."

"Why be so mysterious about it?" chaffed James.

"Don't tease him," said Alice. "I expect it's something harmless. Let him go, Mum."

Mrs Appleby smiled. "As long as you're not getting into mischief," she said. "But mind – only five minutes. It's your bed-time."

"Five minutes will be quite enough," smiled Sam. "It's only some secret. I'll explain about it tomorrow if it's worked!" He got up from the table and scampered outside. First he took the dish of dog food from the hole by the hedge and carried it towards the harness room. Every other yard he stopped to put scraps of meat on the ground, laying a trail right to the harness room. Then he took the remaining tit-bit - a juicy ham-bone - from the dish and put it on the bench.

He whistled cheerily. So far - so good. Now to make a dog-shed! He ran to the stable and took an armful of straw from Dapple's bedding. Carefully he spread the straw in a corner of the harness room. Fine! That looked a really cosy bed. What next? Ah, the door!

Expertly, he tested the working of the hinges. They were slightly creaky. To make them work more easily he took the oil-can from the saddle-bag of James's bike, which was in its usual corner, and dropped several spots of oil on the joints. There! That should do the trick.

Next, he lifted a ball of strong twine from the shelf, and cut off a length with his bowie knife. He fastened one end to a hook on the back of the door. Then he took a hammer from the tool chest and drove in a staple, high up on the door post. He threaded the twine through the staple and ran it to one of the big hooks in the ceiling. Finally he cut off the twine leaving a longish piece hanging down, and tied the bone to the end.

"Sam!"

The youngest Appleby groaned as he heard his mother's call.

"Shan't be a moment, Mum," he shouted before putting away the hammer and string and giving the door a final test.

He left the door ajar and ran to the house.

Soon he was curled up in bed, a happy smile on his freckled face. How pleased the Alsatian would be with the bone and his snug bed. It would be grand for the dog to have a home and a master. They would have such fun together – walks, exploring, swimming – Sam's thoughts merged into his dreams and he fell into a sleep that was thronged with island dogs, mystery dogs – but mostly a white Alsatian!

CHAPTER SEVEN

SKIPPER MAKES FRIENDS

"Goodness!" Hannah gasped, jumping out of bed. "What's happening?"

Hannah had been awakened by frenzied barking which sounded slightly muffled as though it came from behind a door. She ran to the window and looked outside.

In the pearly morning light she could see a shape leaping up and down against the glass panes in the upper half of the harness room door. Its head jerked as it barked with ear-splitting insistence. A dog was trapped in there – it was the white Alsatian!

Hannah pushed her feet into her slippers and ran downstairs. James passed her on the way, closely followed by Alice and Mr Appleby who had heard the noise.

"Yes, the white dog's shut in the saddle room," Hannah called to her father as they ran into the farmyard. "Hurry, Dad."

"Now how did that happen?" Mr Appleby mused as he peered through the panes at the growling dog. "I don't see how the door can have blown to."

"Perhaps if we went in to him he'd make friends," Hannah said and grasped the handle of the saddle room door.

"No, don't go in," her father warned. "We'd better leave him for a little while to calm down."

"How did that bone get in there?" puzzled James,

peering into the saddle room. "Never mind, perhaps the dog will settle down and have a good gnaw. Then he'll feel better."

"Meanwhile," suggested Mr Appleby, "how about coming into Castleford with me? We'll grab a sandwich breakfast. I'm due to pick up some calf–food at nine. And while we're there we can report that the dog's locked himself in our saddle room, and is ready to be claimed if his owners turn up."

"Very well, Dad," said James. "What about Sam?"

"Oh, he's still hogging it in bed," declared Hannah. "We can't wait for him."

Meanwhile, at an upstairs window, Sam, still in his pyjamas, crouched behind the curtains, listening to every word. He was counting the minutes until the coast would be clear. Then he would put the rest of his plan into action.

Without bothering to wash – there were more important things to do this morning! – Sam scrambled into his clothes. A few moments later he heard the Land Rover jog down the lane with his father, James, Alice and Hannah aboard. The coast was clear! He ran down the stairs and through the front door. His mother was busy in the kitchen and Gladys, the daily help and dairy-girl had not yet come, so no one saw him. Swiftly he ran round the side of the house and dodged towards the stable block.

Through the harness room door he could see the white Alsatian, prowling round like a caged tiger.

The dog heard the boy and flung himself at the door.

Sam jumped. Golly! The dog was angry –!

Maybe he was still hungry. Perhaps some more food might convince the dog that he was among friends. Sam took some of Laddie's biscuits from a sack. Then he went up the steps outside the stable to the loft above the loose-boxes and the harness room. The Alsatian's barking in the harness room below echoed in the rafters. Sam had never before heard a dog's bark sound so angry. Cautiously he lifted the trap door and looked down.

"Hey, boy," he called softly. "Why all the fuss? I had to lure you in here so I'd have the chance to make friends with you."

The Alsatian bounded round. Suspiciously he stopped barking to listen – and to try to locate – the voice. He saw Sam. He growled, jumping up at the trap door and snapping his jaws. Heavily he fell back, only to jump again.

"Here old fellow –" Sam tried to keep his voice steady but his fingers shook as he threw down the biscuit. "Look, I've brought you something tasty. Oh gosh –"

Before Sam could throw the biscuit the white dog sprang. He leapt on to the bench and bounded through the trap door. Sam fell flat under the impact of the dog's body. The boy let go of the trap door and it clattered down with a bang. The Alsatian and Sam lay near to each other. Sam trembled and did not dare to move. Then the dog, growling suspiciously, backed away and crouched in the dimness of the loft, his glowing eyes fixed on Sam.

Sam lay motionless. For the first time he was scared of the mystery dog. Would the Alsatian attack him? He held his breath. A minute later the Alsatian stopped growling. Then he padded forward. Sam forced himself to stay quite still while the big dog came nearer. Something about Sam reminded the dog of a boy he had known once, a long time ago – before he was lost. He sniffed Sam's clothes, then his hands. It was all Sam could do not to jerk his hands away. The dog could sense his fear and his hackles rose. Somehow, Sam knew, he had got to reassure the Alsatian, to make him know there was nothing to fear.

"Good dog," Sam said quietly, holding his hands quite still so that the dog would not think he was going to strike him. "Let's be friends." The dog sniffed his face. Sam had a close-up view of sharp fangs.

"Nice old fellow," Sam murmured. "Oh, I wish I knew what you were thinking, but I expect you won't trust me yet because that nasty old plate hit your head, and because I've had to trap you so that we can make friends."

The dog was trying to decide whether Sam meant to harm him. He was still on the defensive although part of him did want to be friends. He had loved that other boy – the one who had been his friend – such a long time ago.

"Good dog!" said Sam, and somehow his voice sounded kindly.

The Alsatian's eyes lost their angry glow, and his hackles dropped. A pink tongue came out and dabbed Sam's nose. Sam squirmed, then chuckled and smiled into the dog's jaws.

"We're chums now!" Sam whooped. "And now I'm going to give you a name! I thought it up last night. It's Skipper! Yes, Skipper because you live in an old boat!"

Gently he put up his hand to stroke the dog's white ruff. The Alsatian's growl came again but died in his throat. His tail moved in a doubtful way. Sam grew bolder. He patted the dog's head and tickled him under the chin. The dog's tail began to swing. Sam's eyes took on a hopeful gleam. The dog was going to be friends.

"Skipper! Oh, Skipper!" Sam murmured happily.

The dog wagged. He seemed to like to be called by a special name, Sam thought.

"Sam!"

The dog's ears pricked at Mrs Appleby's shout. Sam groaned.

"Sam!" Mrs Appleby called again. "Breakfast's ready!"

"Come on, old chap," Sam stood up and looped his tie round the Alsatian's neck. "Let's show Mother what good pals we are."

"Woof!"

Sam impulsively hugged the dog who went limp in his arms and rolled over to have his tummy tickled.

"Oh Skipper!" gasped Sam. "You've been longing to be friends with me just as I have with you. What fun we'll have!"

Mrs Appleby gasped in amazement as Sam led the dog into the kitchen.

"Your Dad told me the dog was in the harness room, and that he was very wild," said Mrs Appleby. "However did you manage to calm him down?"

Sam smiled at his mother in triumph.

"Skipper and I understand each other," he said. "We're the best of friends."

"So it's Skipper is it? Well, he seems to like his name." Mrs Appleby blinked in surprise as she watched Sam feeding the white Alsatian on scraps of bacon. "Now don't give him all your breakfast. I haven't time to cook any more. Today's wash day don't forget."

"Sorry Mum." Sam grinned cheerfully. "Skipper's nearly forgotten what real food tastes like. He's only had the few scraps Hannah saved for him since he was shipwrecked."

"Well, try him on Laddie's biscuits," his mother suggested. "Sailors are used to hard tack." She gazed at the hungrily eating dog and dipped a piece of bread into her egg as a special titbit for him. "I wonder if he likes porridge."

So, to the amazement of the other Applebys when they came back from town a few minutes later, Skipper was standing in front of the kitchen fire, lapping porridge and milk from an old pudding dish.

"Wonders never cease!" James gasped, staring from the Alsatian to his mother and Sam. "So you've tamed our wild dog from the sea."

"All done by kindness," Sam grinned. "Meet Skipper!"

"Good for you, Sam," said James.

"And a jolly good name for the dog!" decided Alice.

"I wonder if he'll let us stroke him," Hannah said, edging nearer the dog. "Oh yes, he loves it!"

"And he answers to his name," said Sam after the dog had finished eating. "Watch! Skipper - here boy!"

Tail wagging, the dog looked up from his food and trotted towards his new friend.

"Skipper, come on," James tried.

"Skipper!" called Alice. "Come here!"

But it was with Sam that the Alsatian stayed, sniffing the boy's shoes.

"Of course he won't come to you," Sam explained stroking the dog. "You see, I tamed him and showed him how much more snug he would be in our harness room than under that old boat."

Hannah was about to protest: "But I saw him first! I ought to have some share in him until we find the owner."

Then she thought that would sound selfish so she tried to smile and show she was pleased that the dog was no longer savage.

"Right now," Sam said, getting up from the table, "Skipper and I are going for a walk. Coming, Hannah?"

"Oh yes. Thanks, Sam," Hannah said eagerly.

She was glad that Sam seemed willing to share Skipper.

Soon the dog would get used to them all. He would be their chum – a dog they could take rabbiting and boating, the kind of pet they had longed for and never had.

Of course there was loyal and faithful Laddie. But he belonged to the farm and was needed there. As Dad had often said, a working sheepdog was happier sticking to his job and taking pride in it than in being made too much of a pet.

They loved Laddie – and always would – but he was not their very own dog as she hoped the white Alsatian would be. Hannah stroked Skipper and gazed into his bewildered eyes.

"Skipper," she said softly, "please stay and be our dog."

"Until his real owner turns up," said Alice.

"I'd forgotten about that," sighed Hannah, and went strangely quiet before she added: "Perhaps he won't come for some time. Or perhaps he might never come!"

CHAPTER EIGHT
ADVENTURES WITH SKIPPER

Later that day Skipper bounded ahead of the children as they ran across the fields to the headland. He sniffed at clumps of gorse and heather and investigated every rabbit scrape and track.

"There's a warren," Alice told Sam, pointing to a sandy bank in which she could see a score or more rabbit holes. "I wonder what he'll make of them."

"Skipper!" Sam called. "Over here." He waved his arm towards the rabbit warren. "Seek!"

They watched the Alsatian scrabble at the hole until his velvety white face was dusky with soil.

"He's a keen rabbiter," said Alice. "I wonder if he's good at tricks, too."

"We know he can beg," said James. "Let's see what else he can do." He held out his arm and called to the dog. "Here, Skipper."

Skipper withdrew from the burrow, but he glanced to Sam for orders before trying to understand what James meant him to do.

"Jump, Skipper," Sam said, holding out his arm as James had done.

But apparently the trick the Alsatian knew was a different one. Skipper ran to Sam, leapt for his arm and held it quite gently in his jaws, at the same time wagging his tail as though to let Sam know that it was a game.

"Look, everybody!" Sam shouted. "He's showing me that he's been trained to hold."

"That's it," agreed James. "Somebody must have given him guard-dog training."

"Isn't he clever?" Hannah gazed admiringly at Skipper who had now released Sam and was sitting obediently at the boy's feet, ready for the next 'game.'

"Let's see if he can find my hanky," Alice suggested hiding her handkerchief in a clump of bracken.

"First he'll have to be given a clue," said Sam, handing the dog one of Alice's hair ribbons to sniff. "Seek, boy." Skipper bounded forward and began to quarter the ground. Then he ran towards a stick. He picked it up and trotted to Sam, putting the piece of wood on the ground near his young master, backing a few paces away and waiting, tail swinging, in happy anticipation that Sam would pick up the stick.

"His training hasn't gone as far as hanky finding," Hannah chuckled. "But he seems to know another game. Go on, Sam. Throw it for him."

Still playing the stick-game with Skipper, the four children made their way across the headland.

"Let's go down to the cove," Hannah suggested.

Skipper barked, as though he, too, thought it was a good idea.

The white dog eagerly ran ahead, picking his way between the rocks, sniffing at the crevices, and watching small crabs scuttle under the rocks.

"Look!" Hannah pointed when they reached the beach. "Old oil drums washed up by the sea. Let's make a 'wall' of them for Skipper to jump."

"Wizard idea!" Sam whooped as he scampered towards the oil drums with Skipper bounding delightedly beside him.

Skipper was wonderful, Hannah thought. He was full of fun, intelligent and game for anything.

"Lend a hand, Alice," Hannah called to her sister, hurrying to help Sam with the drums.

The four Applebys took off their sandals and waded through a shallow stretch of water to reach the three oil-drums which had been stranded on a sand-bank. With Skipper splashing noisily beside them, they got the drums ashore and set them up in a row.

"Now Skipper –" Sam ordered as he showed the dog the drums. "Jump!"

Skipper pricked his ears and stood alert, but did not jump.

"Go on!" urged Sam.

The dog held his head to one side, puzzled.

"He doesn't understand," said Alice. "Throw the stick over for him, Sam."

"Right," Sam hurled the stick over the row of drums. "After it, Skipper."

Skipper dashed forward, scuffing up the sand as he ran. He swerved, dodged round the drums and galloped on to pick up the stick.

"He's too clever for you, Sam," chuckled James.

"Let's stand at the sides of the drums," suggested Hannah.

"Then he won't be able to run out. He'll have to go over."

But Skipper already had other ideas. Stick in mouth, he trotted to the water's edge. Then he put the stick down on the sand and stood there, barking as if to say: "Come on, Sam. I know a better game. Throw this stick out to sea and I'll bring it back to you!"

Sam hurled the stick beyond where the waves broke. With a bound, Skipper sprang through the foam. He waded shoulder deep and swam strongly towards the piece of wood. He seized it between his teeth, and turned, his tail swinging like a rudder. His paws paddled for the shore and his head and neck were outstretched to get to Sam all the sooner.

"Jolly good!" said James.

"Clever dog!" Alice patted the Alsatian as he came ashore, water dripping in rivulets from his fur.

She jumped aside when Skipper shook himself, sending water over her.

"Look quickly!" said Hannah, "See a rainbow in the spray from Skipper's coat."

"I missed that," said Alice.

"Let me throw it this time, Sam," James asked. "And I'll send it right out."

"Very well," Sam agreed.

"Don't miss Skipper's rainbow this time, Alice,"

said Hannah.

"After it, Skipper," shouted Sam as the stick went whizzing over the waves.

Skipper swam out. Then he seemed to catch sight of something farther out to sea. The children watched in surprise. This time Skipper swam right past the stick.

"Skipper!" shouted Hannah. "You've missed it. Seek over!"

But the Alsatian still paddled on – straight out to sea.

"Skipper!" called Alice.

James whistled.

"Skipper!" Sam bellowed. "Oh, why don't you come back?"

"Look! He's swimming after that fishing smack," Hannah gasped. "Oh Skipper do come back!" Skipper heard the shouts but he could not turn back just then – not even for the children whom he was growing to love. Out to sea was a big boat, and something in Skipper's doggy brain connected ships and boats with his master. He half thought that if he could reach the boat he might find his master aboard. So he just paddled on determinedly. But the more he swam the farther away the boat seemed to go. He must swim faster!

Faster – and even faster!

If only he could reach it! But even though he swam as hard as he possibly could the distance between him and the fishing smack widened. He would never reach the boat. He knew that in his heart, but he would not give in. His doggy spirit would not be beaten.

Gallantly he went on swimming even though the current was against him. His paws ached. Salt water splashed into his mouth as he opened his jaws to pant. He could not get his breath and his lungs felt as though they would burst. Yard by yard he swam, painfully now, no longer able to breast the waves, the crests of which were breaking over his head and filling his eyes and nose with stinging salty water.

"Skipper!" Sam yelled from the shore as the dog disappeared from sight. "Skipper!"

Sam's voice choked. He was nearly in tears.

Concern for the dog showed on the faces of all the children. Would he be able to swim back to the shore?

"I'll keep on calling." Sam took a deep breath. "Skipper! Look – oh, he's turning round!"

As the children waded into the water they saw Skipper stop swimming. He seemed caught in the current and swept back for a few yards. Actually he had lost consciousness for a moment as a big wave battered into his face, but the children did not know that.

When Skipper came round again he felt dazed and very tired. He blinked at the fishing boat, so far away now, that even he had to admit it was hopeless to try to reach it. He felt the current pulling him. His paws would not carry him on any farther. His whole body became limp.

The waves broke over his head, and exhausted and helpless, he drifted on the current out to sea.

CHAPTER NINE

SKIPPER IS CLAIMED

"Skipper!" Sam yelled, cupping his hands in a desperate effort to make himself heard. "Good dog! Here!"

Skipper heard the boy's shout only faintly, as though from another world. There it was again! He remembered that even though he had not been able to reach the boat where he hoped to find his old master, he still had friends on shore. With a superhuman effort he turned towards the beach and began swimming slowly. The shore seemed a long way off – almost as far as the boat had been. Would he ever be able to reach it? But he must! He must – answer the call of his young friend.

"Skipper!" Sam called again.

The dog's eyes were fixed on the small figure of the boy who was knee deep in the sea. The sight gave him new strength. He struck out gamely. But his new strength did not last. He was so tired and his brain felt muzzy from the continual pounding of the waves. All he wanted to do was to give up the struggle, to sink down, and let the waves close over him ...

"Skipper!" Sam's voice sounded nearer this time. "Good boy! You've nearly done it! Come on, Skipper, please try again."

The mists parted. Skipper saw the shore clearly again. It was getting nearer. He weakly paddled his paws. A big wave came up behind him and lifted him nearer shore. He was now out of the current and the tide was carrying him towards the beach. His friends had waded out to greet him.

James, knee deep in the sea, was the first to grab the dog by the loose skin at the back of his neck.

"His eyes are shut and he's almost unconscious," James said urgently, holding the dog's head above the waves. "Come on, everybody. Lend a hand to get him out."

Skipper's tail threshed the water feebly as he felt the children's gentle hands on him. They dragged him through the water. His dangling paws at last touched the firm sand and thankfully he staggered to the shore, with some help from the Applebys. He flopped on to the wet sands, and as he lay his flanks heaved while he tried to cough up the salt water that he had swallowed.

"Skipper, oh, Skipper!" Sam murmured, kneeling beside the dog. "You came back to me!"

Slowly Skipper lifted his head. His pink tongue fondly dabbed Sam's chin. He was glad to be back with the children who loved him. He lay at Sam's bare feet and panted exhaustedly, trying to get back his strength.

"Poor old Skipper!" Hannah soothed as she stroked his head.

After a while Skipper's coughing and panting stopped, and he was again breathing easily. He stood up gamely, and his eyes turned to Sam as though to say: "What do you want me to do now?"

"Ready to go on, old chap?" James asked, buckling on the dog's lead. "Come on then. We'll take you home so that you can have a really good rest."

Alice broke into a run.

"I'm going ahead to warm him some milk."

Skipper walked slowly back to the farmhouse, shivering and rather sorry for himself. But he cheered up when he had lapped up the warm milk that Alice had prepared for him. The milk soothed his throat which felt sore from all the sea-water he had swallowed, and the warmth put new strength into his tired limbs. All the same he was glad just to lie on the kitchen floor where the red tiles were warmed by the sun that streamed through the open doorway.

"It's lovely to have you safely back, Skipper," Hannah sighed, sitting where she could watch the sleeping dog. "If we'd lost you in the sea – oh goodness, but it doesn't bear thinking about! You're safe now and that's all that matters!"

Next day a light blue sports car drove into the farmyard at lunch-time, just as the Applebys were starting on second helpings of ginger pudding.

A tweed-clad man got out of the car and walked to the door.

"Good afternoon," James greeted the stranger, opening the door.

"You'll be Mr Appleby, junior," smiled the man,

deciding that James was too old a boy to be called Master Appleby. "My name's Taylor. The police told me you'd found a white Alsatian."

"Yes, we have," James nodded, suddenly getting a sinking feeling.

"Somebody to claim Skipper!" Hannah whispered in dismay to her sister.

"This would have to happen," groaned Alice, "just when, somehow, we've grown to regard Skipper as our own dog."

"May I see whether he's my dog? That is – if it is convenient?" Mr Taylor asked James politely.

James gulped. His mouth felt dry. He tried to smile at the man.

"Of course." He held the door open. "Come in, Mr Taylor," Mr Taylor nodded briefly to Mrs Appleby and the three other children before he looked long and eagerly at Skipper who stood by the hearth, tail ready to wag if the man spoke to him.

"Are you sure he's you dog, Mr Taylor?" Mrs Appleby asked. "He doesn't seem to know you."

"I don't think he remembers me." Mr Taylor held out his hand to Skipper. "Here boy. Here, Patch!"

Skipper wagged, and slowly went towards him and sniffed the outstretched hand. Was this some-body with whom the children wanted him to be friends?

"I wouldn't say he really recognises you," James said politely. "He just senses that you're a visitor who likes dogs. He didn't even know the name that

67

you called him."

"Somehow I think he does remember me," Mr Taylor asserted, stroking Skipper's velvety white head. "Even though he hasn't seen me for three years, and forgotten that he was ever named Patch."

"Three years!" gasped Hannah. "Then he must have belonged to somebody else in the meantime. When we found him he was a castaway who'd swam ashore from a shipwrecked boat."

"That's what we thought," said James. "We couldn't be sure, but he was living under a wrecked dinghy on Bird Island."

"That's interesting," Mr Taylor nodded as he heard the story of Skipper's adventures. "All the same I'm sure he's my dog, even though he might have had another master after I lost him. He always loved the sea, and he might have made friends with some fishermen, and become the dog mascot of some fishing boat."

"Yes, that's possible," admitted James.

"I'd want you to be sure that he is my dog," went on Mr Taylor, taking a printed brochure from his pocket. "Here he is – in a photograph at the kennels where I bought him. I think you'll have to agree that your Skipper is my dog Patch."

The Applebys crowded to see the photograph which showed six white heads blinking over the edge of a basket. The photograph was captioned 'Fine litter of Alsatian puppies' but they looked so much like each other that it would be quite impossible to identify any dog as being one of these puppies now fully grown.

Yet Mr Taylor seemed to think differently.

"There he is – that's Patch," He pointed triumphantly to one of the puppies which had been marked with an 'x' in ink. "He hasn't changed at all, has he?"

"But he might be any of those," Hannah pointed out. "They all look alike."

"Oh no," insisted Mr Taylor. "He still has his dark mark. Look." He pointed to a small shaded patch on Skipper's right ear. "That's why I called him Patch. Oh yes, he's mine, sure enough. Goodness knows where he's been all this time, but I'm quite certain this is the dog I lost on Minton railway-station three years ago when he was just a pup. And the police say that this is the first white Alsatian that's ever been found in the county."

"Will – will you be taking him away now?" Sam murmured dejectedly.

"I'm afraid so," Mr Taylor said, producing a collar and lead from his pocket.

He buckled the collar round Skipper's neck and clipped on the lead. Skipper looked puzzled. Who was this man? Was he going to take him away from the people he had learned to trust? He wriggled, trying to get his head out of the collar.

Mr Taylor tugged at the lead. Skipper sat down.

'Come on, boy," Mr Taylor coaxed. Then he turned to the children. "Perhaps he'll come if you show that you want him to come with me."

Pulled, pushed and dragged by the Applebys, Skipper went unwillingly to the open car. The children hated it all, particularly when Skipper stared at them in hurt bewilderment. They knew he was wondering why they were forsaking him.

"So long, Skipper," gulped Sam. Skipper's ears quivered. The young boy whom he had learned to trust had spoken his name with affection. Maybe the boy did not want to send him away.

Skipper leapt out of the car. Like a streak he ran to hide in the loft, tail between his legs.

"You see, Mr Taylor," said Alice, "he may have been your dog once, but he'll never be happy with you now. I know it must be sad for you, but the fact is that he's quite forgotten you, and now he's got so fond of us that he doesn't want to go with you."

Mr Taylor scratched his head and looked down at Skipper. Then he gazed round at the four children who were anxiously watching his face, trying to guess what he might do next.

"Yes, it does seem as though my puppy's grown up with a will of his own," he admitted, and added impulsively: "Well as you're all so keen to have him, I'll give in. He's yours!"

"Cheers!" whooped Sam. "And more cheers!"

"Oh you are a sport, Mr Taylor!" Hannah exclaimed and, stranger though he was, she felt she could have hugged him.

My Taylor smiled, happy now that he had made

up his mind. "But understand," he told the children, "you must promise to look after him properly."

"Oh we will!" Hannah's eyes shone.

"You bet," promised Sam.

"Then I'll trust him to you," said Mr Taylor. "I'm sure he'll have a good home. I'm making a gift of him to you, and I'll telephone the police-station so that Skipper will be taken off the list of lost dogs."

As Mr Taylor drove away the children ran to the harness room.

"You can come down, now Skipper," Sam called up to the loft trap door. "You're going to stay with us."

When Skipper bounded down he put his arms round the dog's neck, hugging him and whispering into his alert ear: "You're ours, old boy, for keeps! And I bet Dad will be pleased because he thinks as much of you as we do!"

CHAPTER TEN
THE APPLEBYS TRICKED

"Now to make Skipper feel really at home!" exclaimed James.

Getting a lot of fun out of the job, and with their father's consent, the Applebys salvaged the wreck of the dinghy that Skipper had used as a kennel when he was nobody's dog. They patched it up and towed it behind the Curlew to the beach. With much puffing and panting they carried it over the shingle and along the path to the farm.

There, in the cobbled yard, they set it up, keel uppermost, on bricks, to make Skipper an outdoor shelter. Hannah and Alice spent a week's pocket money on a collar and lead and Sam emptied his money box to buy a drinking bowl.

Skipper went with them everywhere, on shopping expeditions to the village, rabbiting on the headland, and for long walks through the woods. But when the children were indoors he sometimes liked to go off on his own, quartering the fields and sniffing the hedgerows. Once he came home, dripping seawater, having swum to Bird Island and back again.

As the weeks passed, Skipper began to make himself useful on the farm, imitating Laddie in rounding up the cows for milking.

Some days later Skipper was snoozing in the long grass of the orchard while the children fed the hens and ducks.

Meanwhile two youths strolled towards the gate that led to the orchard. The first youth was tall and lanky, and the other was short and plump, and they were both smartly dressed. They had just walked down the lane from a van which they had parked on the grass verge.

"There's the dog," the lanky one told his plump friend. "Now don't whistle him. Leave this to me."

"Okay, Alec," nodded the plump youth. "You're the boss."

After peering round to make sure that he was not seen by the children who were busy among the poultry at the end of the orchard, the lanky youth took a handkerchief from his pocket, and slowly waved it over the gate.

"Wait until the dog smells this hanky," Alec told his companion. "He'll be so interested, that he won't be able to help himself. He'll just follow his nose, and you'll be amazed how friendly he'll be."

"Funny how dogs will follow a whiff of aniseed," said the other young man. "It always works." He looked towards the sleek white shape of Skipper who was lying with his nose resting on his paws as he relaxed in the sunshine. "But it doesn't seem to be having much effect on this one."

"It will as soon as the breeze blows the scent in his direction," said Alec, waving the handkerchief back and forth. "Remember how much he liked it last time we treated him to a whiff? There! What did I tell you?"

Skipper stirred from his snooze. His nose twitched, and sniffed the air. His ears went to the alert, and he put his head up to sniff all the better. Now in a flash he was wideawake.

He saw the youths, and a bark rose to his throat. But just then the delightful smell was again wafted on the breeze, and Skipper's bark became only a whimper of delight.

Instead of barking he sniffed deeper and longer. Then it seemed that he had to get nearer to the tantalising aroma. He ambled forward, following his nose.

"There, what did I tell you, Bert?" murmured Alec. "It works like a charm. He was so bewitched he didn't even bark."

"He's a grand-made dog – even fitter than when we saw him before," remarked the other youth, watching the lean, lithe grace of the Alsatian. "Powerful! Just the dog for what we need."

The lanky youth nodded, but did not take his gaze off the Alsatian who, utterly fascinated by the enchanting scent of aniseed, padded, paw after paw, and without hesitation towards the youths.

"If we bought one like him, I reckon we might have to pay a hundred pounds or more," said the lanky youth. "But why pay good money when we can get this one for nothing? Alsatians make the best guard-dogs, and we need a dog to keep pilferers away from our junk yard."

"It was a real brain-wave you had when we saw

him playing with these children and doing his tricks," said the youth called Bert. "Yes, I soon decided he was the dog to keep prowlers away from the yard," agreed the other one. By now Skipper had reached the gate, and, through the bars, was sniffing deep at the aniseed- sprinkled handkerchief. "So you're going to be our dog, eh boy?"

Skipper nuzzled against the lanky youth's hand. His hanky was now in his pocket, but the scent of aniseed still clung to his fingers. The Alsatian did not know what the youths were saying, but their voices had seemed friendly, and that smell – wonderful!

He remembered that he had met these two not long ago, and they had then been kind enough to let him smell the same delightful aroma. Now they were going to give him another little treat.

When the lanky youth was satisfied that Skipper was under the spell of the aniseed he pressed down the latch, and opened the orchard gate.

"Now to claim the dog eh, Bert?" he said with a grin.

"But we've got to use our wits to make these children think that the dog really belongs to us. They aren't fools, and they'll be sure to want proof."

"And I've got it," smiled Bert, tapping his wallet pocket.

"Fine!" said the other one, and with a happily-sniffing Skipper trotting between them as if he had known them all his life, the two youths walked down the orchard path towards the Applebys.

Hannah was the first to see the strangers with Skipper walking obediently at their heels.

"Skipper!" she exclaimed. "What's come over you? Why didn't you bark and let us know we'd got visitors?" She glanced up from the dog and smiled at the two young men. "Are you looking for Dad?"

"Yes," nodded the lanky one. "But if he isn't around, you youngsters will do."

"Hey, James! Alice! Sam!" Hannah called towards the hen pens. "Someone to see us."

A moment later, the two youths, Skipper and the four Applebys stood together in a group under the apple trees.

"Johnson is my name," the lanky youth said, shaking hands with James. "You don't know me, but I know you, and I want to thank you for finding my dog, and for looking after him so well."

There was a moment's thunderstruck silence.

"Did – did you say your dog?" gasped James.

"You must have made a mistake," Alice said in the over-polite tone that she used with people she did not like. "He can't possibly be yours."

"He's my dog," Sam added quietly. "Or rather ours. You see, he was lost by Mr Taylor when he was a puppy, and now Mr Taylor has given him to us."

"Dad knows about it, and so does Sergeant Benson," explained Hannah. "We've bought a dog licence and Mrs Hotchkins at the post office wrote our name on it."

"I see," said the lanky youth and shook his head sadly as though he was sorry for the Applebys. "All the same, buying a dog licence for a dog that isn't yours doesn't mean that you've a claim on the dog, you know."

"But as the real owner gave the dog to us," James explained with a confident smile, "then he's obviously ours, isn't he?"

"He would be" – the lanky youth paused while he looked at all the children in turn – "if he ever belonged to this Mr Taylor. But I'm sorry to have to tell you that Mr Taylor has given you a dog that he never owned. He really is our dog, and we can prove it, can't we, Bert?"

The plump youth nodded. "That's right. Just have a look at this snap."

With sinking hearts, the Applebys crowded round the plump youth who produced a snapshot of Skipper standing beside the lanky youth near the Four Acre field. Skipper's ears were raised alertly and he was sniffing the youth's pocket just in the way that he was doing now.

The Applebys peered closely. There was no doubt about it. The dog in the picture was Skipper, and Skipper's behaviour right now seemed additional proof. He seemed to recognise the youths, and was glad to be near them.

"So Skipper isn't really ours after all," murmured Sam, putting out a hand to touch the dog's neck.

"That's what we're going to find out for sure."

James's voice was quietly determined. He turned to the youths. "When was this snap taken?" The lanky youth stuck out his chin. "This time last year. Why?"

"But no white Alsatian has ever been seen living round here before the last few weeks," put in Alice.

"Quite right, Miss. Skipper wasn't living here," the lanky one nodded. "We brought him when we came on a couple of days' camping holiday with our van. Skipper ran off soon after we'd taken that snap. He went after a rabbit, I reckon. We couldn't find him, and we thought he might have gone back home. But he didn't turn up there."

"Did you notify the police that you'd lost the dog?" asked Alice.

"No, we kept on thinking he might turn up," the lanky one volunteered. "This year we've come here again, hoping we might see something of our dog, and sure enough we heard almost at once that a white Alsatian had been found round these parts."

James scratched his head. "But if he's really your dog, why do you call him Skipper?" he puzzled. "Skipper's a name we gave him."

"And it would be too much of a coincidence for us to have chosen his real name," pointed out Alice.

"Of course it would," readily agreed the lanky youth. "We called him Skipper because that's the name you shouted just now when he came up to us with his tail wagging because he was so glad to see us."

"What's his real name then," demanded Sam, watching the dog closely.

"Rex," said the lanky youth. He dodged back quickly, and clapped his hands. "Come to master, Rex." The dog moved after the youth, still sniffing at his jacket. "See? He answered his name sure enough. Good, Rexy. Come on."

The youth moved away a few paces, and Skipper trotted after him. Bewildered, the Applebys followed.

"Yes, he does seem to know you," admitted Hannah.

"I bet he never took to this Mr Taylor in the way he has to us," said the lanky one.

"Well no, he didn't," said Sam. "But Mr Taylor said he hadn't seen him since he was a puppy."

"He can't ever have been Mr Taylor's dog," Hannah mused sadly.

"Of course he can't," said the lanky youth. "I've had him since he was six weeks old."

With Skipper following them, the two youths set off down the path towards the road where the children could now see a green van parked.

"Thanks for finding Skipper – I mean Rex, and looking after him," the lanky one called over his shoulder. "We'll send you on a reward later."

"We don't want any reward," Alice said in such a quiet voice that it could scarcely be heard.

"Well thanks, anyway."

With that the two youths walked more briskly to

the van. Quite dumbfounded, the Applebys watched Skipper trot loyally to heel behind the young men. Only one thought was in their minds. Skipper was behaving as though he had at last found his real master. And he was so pleased that he had, for the moment, forgotten about them.

"Skipper!" Sam murmured in a small, choked voice. "Aren't you even going to say goodbye."

CHAPTER ELEVEN

SKIPPER STOLEN

The dog paused and looked back at the Appleby children. Then he turned to the youths, sniffed the air and trotted after them through the gate into the lane.

"Up Rex!" called one of the youths when they got near the van.

The children saw the dog jump into a trailer behind the van.

Next moment the engine started and then as quickly died out.

Suddenly James turned to the others.

"There's something very odd about all this," he exclaimed. He thought for a moment. "Of course! why didn't I think of it before? That snap of Skipper near the Four Acre must have been taken within the last few weeks – probably the other day when Skipper went roaming. The picture showed the field under grass. Yet this time last year when those chaps said the snap was taken, I'm sure the field was under wheat!"

"We've been tricked!" Hannah gulped in a voice that trembled with sorrow and anger.

"Golly!" gasped Sam, breaking into a run. "We've got to rescue Skipper somehow. Oh gosh! What ever will Dad say?"

"Can you smell something in the air?" panted James, running headlong.

"Yes – aniseed!" exclaimed Hannah. "That's what dog thieves use to entice dogs. No dog can resist it. Skipper would have to follow. He couldn't stop himself!"

"Oh poor Skipper!" groaned Alice. "He didn't know what he was doing. He just followed the scent, and we've let him be stolen under our very noses."

"Poor Skipper couldn't think about anything except the scent," puffed Sam. "He's the same when he goes after rabbits – just follows his nose!" He choked with rage as he thought of the two scheming youths. "They must have laid a trail of aniseed right to the van. What prize asses we are!"

"And he's not really named Rex at all," gasped Hannah. "They made that up."

At that moment, the van's engine started. The Applebys put on a desperate spurt and ran to the roadway in time to see the green van bouncing down the rutty lane. Between the canvas flaps that partly covered the trailer but swung apart with every bounce, they caught glimpses of an old bedstead and some iron bars.

"Junk dealers, who do dog stealing as a sideline!" James deduced as he sprinted down the road.

The van and trailer rounded the bend, and the canvas began to shake. A doggy nose appeared through the frame of the bedstead and a frenzied barking broke out as Skipper saw them.

Skipper!" yelled Sam. "Jump out!"

The dog seemed to strain forward to obey. Then

something jerked his head backwards and held him tethered in the trailer.

"They must have slipped a rope through his collar," groaned James.

Just then the vehicle rounded the corner and was lost to sight. Gradually Skipper's frantic barking faded into the distance.

"BZY," James panted, memorising the van's registration letters that were chalked on the trailer. "That may be a fake registration but we ought to follow it up. I can't make out any more. The numbers have got rubbed off."

"Anyway, it's a Minton registration," said Sam who, before Skipper had become the main interest in his life, had been a keen car spotter.

"Come on," James decided. He looked at his wrist-watch. "The Minton coach is due at the corner of the lane in just about half a minute! We're going on the war-path right away."

"What luck! There's the van," Hannah pointed breathlessly after they had searched round Minton for some time. "Near those iron railings."

"The railings will be round the yard to keep off trespassers," put in James. He paced towards a square building fronting the pavement. "This must be the office. Let's walk straight in and take them by surprise before they have time to think up any more lies about Skipper."

"They may have made fools of us this time," Alice said hotly, hurrying to her elder brother's side, "but

we'll soon show them what happens when the
Appleby blood is up!''

CHAPTER TWELVE

SKIPPER – COME HOME

James flung open the door of the office to reveal the lanky youth, named Alec, standing with his jacket off and his sleeves rolled up. He was dabbing a handkerchief to his arm, and wincing. When he saw the Applebys he stared in amazement.

"So it's you kids!" he choked. "I ought to claim damages off you. Your dog's just bitten me."

"Hurrah!" exclaimed Sam, unable to contain himself. "Just as I'd hoped ... Hip, Hip..."

"Hurrah!" Hannah joined her younger brother.

"Ah! You said our dog!" echoed Alice. "So you admit it now. Yet you tried to pretend he was yours."

The lanky youth looked sullen. "Well, I can make a mistake, can't I?"

"Where's Skipper now?" demanded James, walking over to the youth.

"How should I know or care?" Alec shrugged. "He bit me then jumped out of the window and ran off."

Hannah went nearer and lifted the hanky from Alec's arm.

"You big baby!" she said scornfully. "The skin isn't broken. It's just bruised. So you can't say Skipper's bitten you. He probably held you. He's been trained to do that."

"Oh, has he?" Alec's voice rose indignantly. "And

that's a nice thing to teach a dog, I must say. Proper dangerous – that is. A dog that bites is against the law."

"So's stealing," Sam retorted. "You only got what you deserved when Skipper bit you – at least when he didn't bite you."

"Yes, you deserve to be eaten by mongrels!" Hannah lingered behind while James, Alice and Sam moved to the door. "You're a common thief. I expect you wanted a dog to guard your scrap yard. Well, you've learnt your lesson and won't try on this trick again."

Leaving the lanky youth gasping, Hannah hurried after the others. "Look!"

She pointed to a scraped-out hollow under the railings. "Skipper's paw-prints," whooped Sam. "He must have burrowed under the railings."

All round the town the children searched, calling Skipper's name, but there was no sight of the dog.

At last they crowded into a telephone box outside the post office to telephone home.

"That you Dad?" James said into the mouthpiece and quickly explained how they had been tricked into letting the white Alsatian be stolen.

"Stay where you are, and I'll come over in the Land Rover," Mr Appleby told them briskly.

Half an hour later when Mr Appleby drew up the Land Rover in the Town Square he found four woebegone children waiting for him. They got into the Land Rover and all started talking at once.

"We've searched everywhere, Dad," Hannah said.

"We followed Skipper's trail as far as the Drill Hall," added James. "After that nobody seemed to have seen him."

"Well, while I'm here," Mr Appleby decided, "we'll have another look."

They toured the outskirts of the town, up one street and down the next, but when dusk began to fall they had still drawn a blank.

"We'll have to get the police on the job, advertise Skipper as being lost and carry on with the search tomorrow," Dad decided, turning the Land Rover towards home.

A gloomy hush settled over the late home-comers. Sam slept with Alice's arms round him.

The Land Rover purred smoothly on, into the village of Sand Beach, over the crossroads, and up the hill to the headland. Soon they were bumping along the drive to the farm.

Hannah gazed forlornly through the windscreen. It was dreadful to come home without Skipper. She imagined how it had been on other days - happier days when they had all gone for picnics in the Land Rover. Skipper had been beside them, his paws on the back of the front seat, craning to get the first sight of the farm, as pleased as they were to be home. Hannah gulped. Wiser not to think about that, because one would give way to a flood of tears, and then be ashamed.

Suddenly she sat upright and peered into the falling

darkness. Across the field near the farm was a white shape. It was moving slowly and it looked footsore. She stared. Surely it couldn't be – Yes, it was!

"Skipper!" shouted Hannah. "Look, he's found his own way home. Stop Dad!"

Sam jerked awake at the excited cries. He rubbed his eyes and blinked round sleepily while the other children jumped down on the drive. Then he saw what they were excited about. Loping towards them over the moonlit meadow was a weary, white Alsatian.

"Skipper!" murmured Sam. "Gosh! I hope I'm not dreaming."

The dog's limping trot changed to a swift-footed run. With a yelp he hurled himself on Sam who had jumped down from the Land Rover. Next he ran whimpering to Hannah, bunting her on the nose as he leapt to lick her face. Then it was Alice's and James's turns. Lastly Skipper went to Mr Appleby and lay at his feet, making whimpering noises in his throat while his tail thumped the ground.

"Skipper, you're a dog in a million." Mr Appleby looked straight into the dog's glowing eyes. "A really loyal, 'come home' dog."

At the word 'home', Skipper leapt in the Land Rover and stood, forefeet planted firmly on the back of the front seat, tongue lolling, bright eyes peering through the darkness, eager to glimpse the friendly farmhouse again.

"You're as pleased to be back as any of us,

Skipper," Hannah said, hugging him and pressing her cheek against the soft fur on his neck. "You're a good, faithful dog, Skipper, and you know Headland Farm is your home. You'd never want to leave us, would you?"

CHAPTER THIRTEEN
LADDIE NEEDS THE VET

"What can we do today?" Sam turned to his mother as he got up from the breakfast table. "Skipper doesn't seem to want to go far from home, so I think we'd better stay round the farm."

"Well, if you'd like to help," suggested Mrs Appleby, "There's a job in the apple loft, washing down the apple trays and setting them to dry, ready for the early crop."

"Coming, Skipper?" Alice asked the dog.

She turned to the white Alsatian who was watching to see what they would do next.

Skipper lay down on the rug and dropped his nose on to his paws, making it clear that he was not moving from the farmhouse kitchen just yet.

"Oh well, we'll go without you then," said Sam. "I expect you want to spend the day snoozing, you old sleepy-head."

The children went off to clean and stack the apple trays.

Meanwhile Mr Appleby, unknown to the youngsters, was in the cowshed, bending down to Laddie who was sitting on the cobbles, paws raised, with a 'please-make-it-better' expression in his eyes.

"Hullo!" exclaimed Mr Appleby. "It isn't often you're in trouble, Laddie." He knelt beside the farm dog. "What's wrong?"

Mr Appleby's fingers felt between the small

cushion-like pads on the dog's paws.

"Now what is it? A bit of stone, or a thorn? Hm! I can't find anything."

Laddie whimpered as though to say "Of course you can't. You're looking in the wrong place."

Laddie rolled over on his side, and threshed one of his front legs in the air.

"Ah! So this is the trouble." The farmer's touch was very gentle as he felt for the injury. "You've torn a dew claw rather badly, perhaps on a bramble. I suppose it's painful when it catches on anything. Well, we'll soon put that right." "Woof!" asked Laddie, which in dog language might have meant: "How?"

"You leave that to me, Laddie." The farmer walked to the cow shed door. "Just lie there and rest your paw. No work for you today."

A few minutes later, Mr Appleby was speaking on the telephone.

"Headland Farm here," he said, after dialling the number of the veterinary surgeon who always attended to the ailments of the farm animals. "Is Mr McNab there?"

"Mr McNab and his wife are away on a few days' holiday," answered a man's voice at the other end of the phone. My name's Baxter. I'm a fully qualified relief vet. Mr McNab's called me in to take over his work while he's away. Can I help you?"

The farmer quickly explained about Laddie.

"Right!" said Mr Baxter. "I'll pick up the dog,

and remove the dew claw and bandage the paw. I'd rather do it here in the surgery in case it needs to be stitched. I'll come over to take the dog, but I may not be able to manage it until this afternoon."

"That'll be soon enough," said Mr Appleby. "The dog isn't in any pain unless he gets among the brambles so I'm keeping him around the yard."

"Yes, very wise. Well, I'll be calling on you later, Mr Appleby. Goodbye."

That morning, the relief vet found that his other visits to sick animals did not take him very long, so he was able to call at Headland Farm in the morning instead of the afternoon.

The farm seemed deserted as he drove his car into the yard. Laddie, the patient, having been excused farm duty, was sleeping deeply on a pile of straw, and so did not bark a warning. Mr Appleby, not expecting the relief vet until the afternoon, was mending fences in the far meadow. The children were still busy in the apple loft, and Mrs Appleby was at the far end of the kitchen garden, picking some peas for the midday meal.

Only Skipper was nearby to witness Mr Baxter's arrival in the regular vet's car.

The white Alsatian had woken from his long snooze, and felt frisky, but his tummy told him it was nearly meal-time. He knew that the others would soon come back to the farmhouse. So he decided to sit on the red tiles by the front door, which was ajar, and wait to greet everybody.

Warily, he watched a short, brawny man walk from the car to the door. What did the man want? A low growl rumbled in Skipper's throat as he remembered how the two dog thieves had lured him into a van. Now a strange man had driven up and was walking towards him, and there was no one about to help.

Skipper slunk behind the door. Where were the others? He would feel a lot safer if they were near! Rat-ta-tat! The man was knocking at the door. Skipper lay very still.

Ra-ta-tat!

Skipper tensed. Perhaps the man would go away now. But he pushed open the door.

"Anyone there?" he called.

Skipper knew he was seen. He was about to growl when the stranger's voice suddenly became friendly.

"Hullo, old boy," said the vet. "So you're the dog who's torn a dew claw. Mr Appleby said you'd be around the farm. Now you come with me in the car and I'll take you to the surgery, fix up your paw and soon have you back here."

Reassured by the gentle voice, Skipper padded forward and sniffed the man's jacket. Before he knew what had happened, Mr Baxter had slipped a cord through his collar, and was leading him towards the car.

He opened the door.

"In you go!" Mr Baxter bade cheerfully.

He did not notice that the dog was baring his fangs.

CHAPTER FOURTEEN
A DOG'S DISGRACE

Skipper stood firm. Now he was sure. Friendly and gentle-voiced though this man was, he was trying to steal him. It had happened before. Skipper had once allowed himself to be lured away. But he was not going to let it happen again. He barked to let the family know his plight.

"Maybe you're thinking your paw will hurt if you jump into the van," murmured the vet, thoroughly trusting Skipper because of his docile behaviour so far. "Now if I just lift you in –"

The vet's nimble hands closed round Skipper's chest. The dog's eyes glowed in fear and anger. So he was going to be stolen. And no one was coming to the rescue. Well, he would have to fight his own battle. Why should he let anyone do this to him? He was a big dog, and could defend himself. Suddenly he wriggled from the vet's grasp. He showed his teeth, snarled, let out a wild bark, and flung himself at the astonished man.

Hearing Skipper's barking, Laddie limped from the cowshed, saw the vet's car, recognised it, and stood beside it with his paw raised waiting for it to be made better.

Hannah ran to the loft window and rubbed a hand over the cobwebby pane so that she could look out.

"It's the vet's car," she reported. "He must have

come about Laddie's dew claw. But it isn't Laddie barking – it's Skipper!"

"Stop that, Skipper!" James gasped, appalled by what he saw from the other window. The relief vet lay motionless on the cobbles. Skipper, with his paws on the man's chest, and his teeth in the vet's jacket sleeve was holding him down.

Standing nearby on three paws was Laddie, watching Skipper's behaviour in shocked surprise.

"Oh gosh!" exclaimed Hannah as they all ran to the rescue. "Mr Baxter's never been to the farm before, and he must have though Skipper was the farm dog who had to go to the surgery. And Skipper must have thought he was being stolen!"

"Skipper!" Sam yelled. "Let go."

But Skipper did not understand. He thought he was doing the right thing. He remembered how strangers had lured him away in a van. Well, he would not let himself be stolen. Grr! Not likely!

As the children dashed up, Mr Baxter slowly sat up, looking dazed. There was a lump where his head had struck the car door when Skipper had attacked him. The blow had momentarily knocked him out. Now he was coming round, and although still muzzy in his head, he was tough and game. Deftly, he shot out a sinewy hand, and grasped Skipper's tail, lifting the dog's hind legs off the ground.

The enraged, fear-stricken dog tried to yelp a protest and in doing so opened his jaws and released the man's sleeve.

With the hand that was now free, the new vet grabbed Skipper by the collar and held on tightly.

"Got him!" he exclaimed to the children. "There's a muzzle in the back of the car. Hurry! He's nearly twisting my arm off."

Sam found the muzzle which Mr Baxter quickly slipped over Skipper's jaws and tightened the strap.

"Are you hurt?" Alice asked, taking Mr Baxter's arm in case he needed support. "I say, we're dreadfully sorry this happened."

"Maybe it was my fault," said Mr Baxter, and looked towards Laddie in the car. "I got the wrong dog. That's the one with the torn dew claw. All the same, I must say, this fellow gave me a nasty shock. Believe me, I've met bulls who've been more pleased to see me!"

"Skipper's not really treacherous," Sam declared, holding the dog's collar as Skipper whimpered into his muzzle. "He thought you were stealing him."

Grr!

Skipper evidently still thought so to judge from the growl that he managed to make behind the muzzle.

CHAPTER FIFTEEN
HIDE-AWAY!

"Don't be sad, Skipper," Hannah murmured soothingly a little later. "When the vet's gone, Dad will take off that nasty old muzzle, and then you and I will go for a scamper on the sands."

Skipper's whimpering faded away. He pressed himself near to the girl and his tail began to wag. Just then Hannah shivered. A chill hush had crept over the farmyard. No hens cackled. The other children were silent for once. Even the murmur of Dad's and Mr Baxter's voices from the half open sitting room window above her had stopped.

Then – quite loudly and nearer the window – came Dad's voice. He did not know his younger daughter was there because he could not see her below the window frame.

Hannah's smiles faded and tears pricked her eyes, as thoroughly shocked, she realised what Dad and Mr Baxter were planning.

"I don't like it, Baxter," Dad was saying. "No more than you do. But you're right. For the children's sake, we've got to do it. With children around, we can't take the risk of keeping a dog that might turn vicious at any moment."

"It's going to be sad for them, but they needn't know that I'm going to put him to sleep," said the vet. "You might explain that he's going to another farm somewhere. That might be kinder."

"And I'll buy them a puppy," Hannah heard her father say. "That'll help them forget poor old Skipper." The farmer's voice was very quiet, but loud enough for Hannah to hear every word in sick horror. "The children don't seem to be around just now. Well, I suppose we'd better get it over. I'll give you a hand with the dog. I'd want to be with him at the end so that he won't feel forsaken."

Hannah heard the men's footsteps cross to the door. Though tears were welling in her eyes, and her lips were trembling, her chin was tilted in determination. With shaking fingers, she loosened Skipper's collar and slipped it off his head.

"They shan't put you to sleep, Skipper. You're not a vicious dog." Her small voice shook. "You won't bite anyone again – ever! Oh, you must be given another chance."

The collar was off. Then the muzzle. Skipper was free.

"Quick, boy – oh quick!" she whispered and as she heard the rattle of the door knob, she grabbed the muzzle and ran round the corner of the house.

The dog loped beside her, mystified by the strange urgency in her voice. Some instinct told him that he must obey her. He followed her into the stable, and sat tensely by the door, waiting for his next orders as Hannah hurriedly saddled Dapple.

Round the next corner, in the yard, the farmer and Mr Baxter gazed at the empty dog collar at the end of the tethered chain.

"He's slipped his collar and made off," declared Mr Baxter. "Now what did I tell you? You'll always have trouble with that dog, Mr Appleby. Goodness knows what injury he might do if he runs amok."

Mr Appleby grunted unhappily.

As soon as the farmer and the relief vet went down the drive in search of Skipper, Hannah, in the stable, gave the dog a comforting pat.

His warm wet tongue gratefully dabbed her hand. Somebody loved him.

"There, old chap. We'll win through somehow." She grasped Dapple's reins, and peeped out of the stable door to see that the coast was clear. "Now to make a dash for it. Hurry, Skipper!"

While the farmer and the relief vet were out of sight behind the elms at the end of the drive, Hannah, astride Dapple, leapt the fence. Skipper jumped a few paces behind them.

Only when they were over the headland did Hannah rein up to look back and listen.

All she could hear was the tinkle of the shingle as it was drawn back by the ebb tide.

"We've got away, Skipper!" she said, and there was triumph in her voice instead of sadness. "Now to hide you where no grown up will ever find you."

Sam goggled, eyes saucer-wide, mouth open, jaw dropped, as he listened to the sensation that the older ones and mother and father were discussing. But they were not telling him everything. They were keeping something back because he was the youngest. But he did know that Hannah, Dapple and Skipper had completely disappeared for some reason or other. They had run away. Why hadn't Hannah let him share this adventure? Perhaps because he hadn't happened to be around.

Well, he would soon put that right. Then he would coax Hannah to tell him why she had run away with the white dog. Unnoticed, he slipped away, down to the paddock, opened the gate and whistled to his Shetland pony, Darkie.

Soon he was on the pony's back, galloping towards the cliffs.

He felt sure Hannah would have taken Skipper to the smuggler's cave. When he came to the cairn of stones which marked the highest point on the headland, he reined up Darkie. He jumped off the pony and made his way on foot along the cliff's edge. Yes, that was the way down. Sam seized the stout stem of a scrub bush, growing on the edge, and swung himself on to the ledge. Nimbly he worked his way along the cliff face towards the crevice which ran down to the mouth of the cave. Hannah must have had a difficult job getting Skipper down, Sam thought.

He glanced down towards the cave. Below lay the sea, pounding round the rocks - a sheer drop of thirty feet. Sam's head swam as he gazed down. He forced his glance upwards.

He knew he must not look down again. But if he did not, how could he ever find his next foothold?

Sam's legs began to tremble. He gazed up at the rock face. It would be even more difficult to climb up than to go down. His arms were aching now, he knew they would never be strong enough to pull him up the steep part.

"Hannah!" he shouted desperately. "I'm stuck. Come and help me. Hannah!"

CHAPTER SIXTEEN

SKIPPER TO THE RESCUE!

A quarter of a mile away Hannah sat in the underground firing chamber of a disused quarry. She had decided that the smuggler's cave was too dangerous to reach, and so had made for another hiding place.

"I'll bring some straw for your bed here and some food, Skipper." She glanced anxiously round the cramped space. "I do hope you'll be comfortable and won't be lonely –" she broke off, her attention taken by Skipper who was watching the opening, ears quivering.

What had the dog heard? Footsteps? Was somebody coming? Hannah's heart pounded. Protectively she put her arms round the dog. He whimpered and this time she heard the sound that was upsetting him – a far away human cry carried on the wind.

Skipper barked as though to say: "I'm coming."

He ran through the opening and bounded up the quarry side on to the heather-covered turf of the headland. Hannah panted after him and peered over the edge. There was Sam, white-faced, stranded on a jutting rock, fifteen feet below. He looked up and saw his sister.

"I can't get up, Hannah." Sam's voice trembled. "I'm stuck!"

"Gosh Sam!" Hannah gasped when she saw his plight. "Don't move."

While Hannah was trying to decide what to do, Skipper intrepidly dashed to the rescue. He disappeared over the cliff, miraculously leaping on to a ledge that jutted out above the steep rocks and foaming sea below.

"Go back, Skip!" Sam ordered, afraid that the dog might fall to certain death.

But Skipper just fixed his eyes on another ledge and sprang. Leap by leap the dog made his way down the cliff to the boy.

Hannah hardly dared to breathe. Skipper was now on a rock that was just below Sam.

"Now, Sam," Hannah called, when Skipper was just level with the boy's hands. "Move your grip to Skipper's collar. He'll help you on to the ledge."

Skipper and Sam crawled to safety and both lay on the ledge, the Alsatian licking Sam's face.

"Stay there and don't move," Hannah called. "I'm going for the coast-guard."

"Skipper saved my life!" Sam panted to Mr Fellows, the coast-guard, who soon got the boy to the top with the aid of ropes. "They can't take his life away now."

Hannah turned pleadingly to the coast-guard.

"Now is it fair, Mr Fellows?" she implored. "Skipper isn't the type of dog who turns deliberately vicious."

"What exactly happened?" asked Mr Fellows, sitting down on the soft grass on the hill-top while Skipper lay at his feet. "I can't give an opinion until

I've heard all the facts, you know."

When Hannah and Sam had told him absolutely everything and some things twice over, Mr Fellows got to his feet.

"Well, I'm prepared to put in a good word for the dog," he declared. "But you'll all have to go home, you know, so you may as well let me take you now, and I promise I'll do my best for Skipper."

Half an hour later, the Appleby children and the white Alsatian waited in the orchard while their mother and father, Mr Fellows and the relief vet discussed Skipper's fate, in the farmhouse sitting room.

The suspense was dreadful. Then after a little while, Mrs Appleby came out, and whistled for Skipper.

The children watched the dog run trustingly into the farmhouse.

"Maybe they're going to see how he behaves with Mr Baxter now Skipper knows that he's really a friend, and not a dog thief," James said to cheer up the others. He climbed up an apple tree to get a view of the front door. "Yes, that's it! Skipper's trotting to the vet's car, and they're all watching. He's letting Mr Baxter get in. Now Mr Baxter's leaning over to pat Skipper."

"Skipper! Oh Skipper!" Sam suddenly shouted. "You've shown them all that you're a dog to be trusted."

At the sound of Sam's voice calling him, Skipper

bounded, tail wagging, to the orchard.

"James! Alice! Hannah! Sam!" came Mrs Appleby's voice from the farmhouse door, and by her cheerful tone they knew it was good news that she had for them. We're going to keep Skipper! We're all convinced he's not really a dangerous dog."

"Hurray!" The four Applebys joined hands and danced round a bewildered but pleased Skipper. "Hurray!"

They were still dancing when their mother and father appeared through the orchard.

Mrs Appleby took her husband's arm and smiled into his eyes, proud of the loyalty that her children had shown to Skipper – and proud, too, of the dog who had saved the youngest one.

"You see, dear, Skipper's not only a life-saver," she said softly, "but he's one of the family."

"Yes, he's our dog sure enough," said Mr Appleby, and at the sound of his master's voice, the white Alsatian dodged between the children's dancing feet, and trotted to the farmer's side.

Mr Appleby tickled him behind the ears so that he squirmed with pleasure. Then, in a voice that was so quiet that only the dog heard, the farmer added: "Our own Skipper!"

Also published by Cavalier Paperbacks:

I Rode A Winner *by Christine Pullein-Thompson*

The Lost Pony *by Christine Pullein-Thompson*

For Want of a Saddle *by Christine Pullein-Thompson*

Stolen Ponies *by Christine Pullein-Thompson*

A Pony in Distress *by Christine Pullein-Thompson*

Horse and Dog Stories

Hamish *by Joanna Cannan*